A MESSAGE FROM THE GRAVE

"I'm looking for Miss Carrie Kittrick," the rider said.

The maid looked at his dusty clothes and his beard stubble and asked disapprovingly, "Who will I tell her is calling?"

"She wouldn't know my name. Tell her her uncle sent me."

A girl of medium height wearing a dress the color of her blue eyes came to the door and looked at him.

"Name's Hanaway, ma'am."

"I don't believe my uncle sent you. You're making it up—my uncle is dead."

"I know, ma'am. I helped bury him."

Bantam Books by Luke Short
Ask your bookseller for the books you have missed

AMBUSH
FIDDLEFOOT
FIRST CLAIM
HARDCASE
HARD MONEY
MAN FROM THE DESERT
RAIDERS OF THE RIMROCK
SILVER ROCK
THE SOME-DAY COUNTRY
SUNSET GRAZE
VENGEANCE VALLEY

Three for the Money

LUKE SHORT
MAN
FROM THE
DESERT

BANTAM BOOKS · TORONTO · NEW YORK · LONDON

MAN FROM THE DESERT

A Bantam Book / November 1971
2nd printing ...... January 1972   3rd printing .... June 1979

ISBN 0–553–12558–3

Published simultaneously in the United States and Canada

Bantam Books are published by Bantam Books, Inc. Its trade-
mark, consisting of the words "Bantam Books" and the por-
trayal of a bantam, is Registered in U.S. Patent and Trademark
Office and in other countries. Marca Registrada. Bantam
Books, Inc., 666 Fifth Avenue, New York, New York 10019.

MAN
FROM THE
DESERT

I

The desert now behind him, the big man on the dun leading a pack horse cut across the sparse afternoon traffic of Kittrick's main street and reined in before a man loafing in the archway of the feed stable.

"I'm looking for Miss Carrie Kittrick," the rider said. "Know where I can find her?"

The young man in the archway dressed in bib overalls pulled a wooden match out of his mouth past his full mustache and regarded the rider. He saw a man who, if standing in his dusty range clothes, would be tall. His weathered, beard-stubbled and long-jawed face was pleasant enough, his gray eyes patient.

Using his match as a pointer, the man on the ground said, "Go on two blocks, then look to your left. Big frame house at the end of the street."

The rider nodded. "You work here?" At the man's nod, the rider held out the lead rope of the pack horse and said, "Take his pack off and grain him."

The hostler accepted the rope and the rider put his dun in motion. As he rode the two blocks, he looked about him. Kittrick seemed a prosperous if dusty desert cowtown with its false-front stores behind tie rails. There was a big box of a frame hotel on the right and a brick bank on the corner where he left the main street.

Ahead of him now, perhaps two blocks distant, he saw the huge frame house that was almost hidden by tall oleander hedges and cottonwoods that towered above all the town's other trees in sight.

The street turned left at the hedges, which here showed a break. As he rode through this break, his horse was on a gravel drive that forked ahead. The right fork curved past the long porch of the two-story, white-painted frame house; the left fork went straight to the outbuildings and stable.

Drawn up at the porch steps was a red-wheeled buggy to which was hitched a dainty black mare. Pacing slowly back and forth by the buggy was a burly man in dark trousers and white shirt.

When he saw the rider head up the curve of the drive dividing a neat lawn on the side that would bring him to the porch, the man halted his pacing and watched. As the rider passed him and nodded, the man said in a surly voice, "Back door, cowboy."

The rider kept on and, when he reached the cast-iron hitching post, dismounted, tied his horse and headed for the porch steps. By this time the servant was standing at the top of the porch steps.

The rider halted on the lower step and the servant asked in the same surly voice, "Anybody here know you? Anybody send for you?"

"No."

"Then back door, like I told you."

"No." the rider climbed the next step.

He seemed to anticipate the kick that was aimed at him, for he dodged to his right, caught the servant's boot and heaved up his leg. Then he lifted the other leg and the man crashed to the floor of the porch on his back with an impact that drove the breath from him in a grunt that was almost a shout.

Swiftly the rider was on the porch, kneeling. He drove his open hand across the servant's face and backhanded him, then lifted him to his feet and shoved him down the steps. Unable to keep his balance, the servant pitched headlong into the rear wheel of the buggy with a violence that skidded the buggy sideways.

The black mare, spooked by the skidding buggy, snorted and set off down the curve of the drive. The servant picked himself off the gravel and set out in pursuit of the runaway, cursing wildly.

The rider watched until buggy and servant vanished behind the hedge, then moved across the porch and twisted the handle of the doorbell set in the door. Moments later the door was opened by a gray-haired Mexican maid in white uniform.

"I'm looking for Miss Carrie Kittrick," the rider said.

The maid looked at his dusty clothes and his beard stubble and asked disapprovingly, "Who will I tell her is calling?"

"She wouldn't know my name. Tell her her uncle sent me."

The maid nodded and gently closed the door in his face.

The rider turned and was looking beyond the drive to the crescent-shaped lawn and flower garden when he heard the door behind him open.

A girl of medium height wearing a dress the color of her blue eyes stood regarding him, her hand still on the doorknob. Her unsmiling mouth was attractively wide under a short nose. Her hair, pinned atop her head, was a tawny, golden color. The rider removed his dusty stetson and came back to the doorway.

"Sarita said you told her my Uncle Jeff sent you," Carrie Kittrick said, still unsmiling.

The rider nodded and said, "Name's Hanaway, ma'am."

"I don't believe he sent you. You're making it up—because my uncle is dead."

"I know. I helped bury him." He reached in the pocket of his dusty jacket, drew out a crumpled letter and extended it, saying, "I think you wrote this to your uncle."

Carrie took the letter, removed the pages from the envelope and scanned them briefly, then raised her glance to Hanaway's long face. "I suppose you've read this on the sly."

"Not on the sly. I read it to your uncle because he was in no shape to."

A look of dismay quickly crossed Carrie's face; she tucked the letter in the pocket of her dress and said swiftly, "You're not to tell anyone in this household about the letter. It was never written."

"If you say so."

They both heard the sound of a horse on the gravel drive. It was the servant returning with the buggy. Carrie turned her head and called inside, "Steve's here with the buggy, Neva."

"Coming," a girl's voice answered back in the hall. They heard footsteps in the hall and then a girl came up beside Carrie and halted. She was dressed for the street, wearing a small hat atop her dark hair. She was a beauty, Hanaway saw, with a smooth, glowing skin; her brown eyes were dark-lashed and melting, as if everything she saw pleased her. She was smaller and younger than Carrie, Hanaway guessed.

Hanaway had stepped aside and Carrie said, "Neva, this is a friend of Uncle Jeff. His name is Hanaway."

Neva nodded politely, murmured the amenities, then stepped out on the porch, saying, "I remembered your list, Carrie."

She gave Hanaway a fleeting smile as she passed him and then the glowering servant handed her down the steps and into the buggy. As he went around the back of the buggy, he raised a fisted hand and shook it at Hanaway, a schoolboy gesture that made Hanaway smile.

"What was that for?" Carrie asked.

"You'll have to ask him."

Carrie shrugged and then said without any warmth, "We can't stand out here all afternoon. Won't you come in?" she turned and led the short way down the hall into a small, book-lined library on the left. The more formal parlor was a big, richly furnished room on the right.

Carrie took one of the two deep leather chairs that flanked the cold fireplace, gestured to the other and then sat down. Hat in hand, Hanaway took the other chair and sat down. He was not going to speak until she made him and she seemed to realize this.

She asked, "Just who are you and what is it you want?"

4

"I worked for your uncle for five years. As to why I'm here, I reckon it's to help you."

"And Uncle Jeff asked you to?" At his nod, she shook her head in bewilderment. "But what can you do to help me?"

"I don't know yet."

Carrie leaned forward, elbows on knees. "You read my letter to Uncle Jeff, you say. Do you remember I asked him to send me a mining lawyer who wasn't known in these parts? Are you a mining lawyer?"

"Not any." Hanaway shrugged.

Then she asked again. "How can you help?"

"Your letter to your uncle said the trouble here is your brother Ben. He's the oldest of you, isn't he?" She acknowledged this with a stiff nod and he went on. "He's wasting the estate your father left the three of you. He's executor so he can do that. You're worried, but Neva isn't because she thinks Ben can't do any wrong. Between the two of them, you're outvoted every time."

Her face was flushed, whether from this invasion of her privacy or anger, Hanaway couldn't tell. She said sharply, "That's what my letter said."

"What's he spending your money on?" Hanaway asked bluntly.

"I don't see that's any of your business," Carrie answered angrily.

"I don't either, but what is he?"

Carrie glared at him a silent moment, then said, "For your information, my brother is president of our bank and of the Kittrick Consolidated Gold Mine. He also manages our other properties. I don't think he's doing a good job of it."

"How's he doing a bad job of it?"

Carrie said in exasperation, "That's what I want a good lawyer to find out. I can't use a—a . . ."

"Unwashed cowboy?" Hanaway suggested.

"You said that, I didn't. But I tell you now, I don't want your help."

Hanaway smiled faintly. "You've got it whether you want it or not."

After a moment of stunned disbelief, Carrie came to her feet. "This is preposterous! I won't let you help, and if you try, you'll get nothing for your pains!"

"I've already been paid." He rose too. "You see, your Uncle Jeff left me his ranch that borders on the mine. There was a condition, though. I was to help straighten out the mess you mentioned in your letter, so I think I'll stick around."

"Not around here you won't. Please leave this house."

He left without another word.

II

At the big, white-painted hotel, Hanaway paid for a week, climbed to the second floor and found his room, a front corner one. Unrolling his blanket roll, which he had picked up at the stable when he had left the dun, he took out a straight-edged razor and a bar of yellow soap.

Stripping off his dusty jacket and shirt, he went over to the washstand and set about shaving. The events of the last half hour puzzled him. Old Jeff Kittrick hadn't paid much attention to his nieces and nephew; they were rich townfolk a long ways away and too busy with their affairs to make the long trip north or to write him regularly. He hadn't envied them their wealth. It was just that he'd never liked their grasping father, his brother, and so had traveled another trail.

Now Hanaway began to understand why. While he'd only met Neva and couldn't judge her, Carrie was something else. There was a streak of arrogance in her that money had probably bred, and then there was her willfullness. His coming had actually angered her. It won't be the last time I make her mad, he thought grimly.

Finished with his shave, he went over to his blanket roll on the bed and took out a clean shirt. As he was unbuckling his belt to tuck in his shirt, he remembered his money belt. He had seven hundred dollars in double eagles hidden there, and a man would be a damn fool to go looking for trouble in a strange country with that much money on him. He emptied the double eagles on the bed, put them in both jacket pockets, strapped on a gun and shellbelt and went downstairs.

7

Outside, he cut across the dusty street, a tall man walking with a certain stiffness that proclaimed he had been long in the saddle.

Entering the bank through open double doors, he saw the clerks' metal-grilled cages on his right. The first window was unattended, but there was a clerk at the second window counting money from a canvas bag under the watchful stare of a waiting townsman.

Hanaway stepped up behind the townsman and was at once aware of raised voices behind the frosted-glass partition that ran the width of the room and was perhaps eight feet high. There were two doors in the partition, the one on the left bearing the gilt legend on its dark oak:

BENJAMIN KITTRICK

PRESIDENT

The voices behind this door were rising in volume now, the sound bouncing from the ceiling and over the partition.

A heavy, assured voice said loud enough for Hanaway to hear it, "You've got no choice, Harry. Every lease in that block has been adjusted."

"That's a fancy way of saying you've sandbagged us," a second voice said angrily.

"You're a lawyer, read your lease," the first voice said, and Hanaway was sure it was Ben's. "It's up for renegotiation at the end of two years. Your second was up yesterday."

"Will you build me a second story? I'll need to rent out rooms to make my new rent."

"No," Ben said coldly.

A chair scraped. "The hell with you, Ben. The—hell—with—you."

A pause, then the door opened. A red-faced and very angry young man in a townsman's pepper-and-salt suit came through the door, not bothering to shut it, and strode past Hanaway.

Now Hanaway saw a big man, perhaps thirty and

8

dressed in a townsman's dark suit, appear in the doorway. He had the same wide mouth as Carrie under a full mustache, but he had Neva's dark eyes and hair.

He halted now and called angrily, "I'll give you a week to get your stuff out of there, Harry."

Harry stopped and turned. "Or you'll what?"

"Throw you out," Ben Kittrick said, then stepped back into his office and closed the door.

The clerk was finished with his customer, who moved toward the lobby door.

"Who just went out—Harry who?" Hanaway asked the clerk.

"Why, Harry Hall. He's a lawyer. Four doors down the next block, this side. Now, what can I do for you?"

Hanaway shelled the double eagles out of his pockets, filled out a signature form, received his deposit slip and went outside.

Heading upstreet, Hanaway considered his idea. Hall was furious with Ben Kittrick and, as he knew from experience, an angry man is seldom a wise man. Maybe Hall could give him information he needed.

Hanaway found Hall's office easily; a sign saying HARRY HALL, ATTORNEY at LAW jutted out a way over the boardwalk. The frontage was narrow; the windows on either side of the handsome walnut door were frosted bottom to top. Hall either liked his own privacy or wanted to protect the identity of his clients. Hanaway tried the door, found it locked, knocked, and was not answered. He turned and looked across the street, where a bold, four-foot-high sign proclaimed BRADY'S, and the wide batwing doors indicated a saloon.

What would a man do who had just lost his lease after a blazing row and now faced eviction? Hanaway pondered. Chances were he'd head for the nearest whiskey to settle him down, and Brady's whiskey seemed the nearest to Hall's office.

In the saloon, Hanaway spotted Hall halfway down the bar which was on the left. A trio of punchers at the bar were drinking it up on their day in town.

Hanaway passed them and moved up to Hall who, cradling a drink in his right hand, looked over at Hanaway with indifference.

Hanaway said mildly, "Mr. Hall, I was in the bank a few minutes ago when you left Kittrick's office. I couldn't help hearing what the row was all about."

Hall had eyes as blue as Hanaway's, and at the moment they were chill and unfriendly. "Is that why you followed me? Why do you care?"

"Maybe I need a lawyer. You are one, aren't you?"

Hall grimaced. "Temporarily, I reckon."

"Can we talk—but not here?"

Hall finished his drink, lifted the glass and said, "I've got some of this stuff in my office. Why don't we go find it?"

He led the way across the street traffic. To Hanaway, following behind, it was obvious that he was at the moment both impatient and disturbed; he spoke absently to riders on the street and people on the sidewalk. Their own greetings, however, seemed warm and friendly, which told Hanaway that this rangy man was liked here.

He unlocked the door of his office and courteously stood aside to let Hanaway walk past him. The office was small, so intimate, so close to the boardwalk that Hanaway understood the frosted glass in the windows. In one glance he took in the roll-top desk, swivel chair, an armchair by the desk and a small sofa against the opposite wall. The far wall held a jammed bookcase flanked by prints of Lincoln and Jefferson. A door to the rear bisected the bookcase.

Hall closed the door, then faced Hanaway. "You know my name, but have I ever seen you before?"

Hanaway said no, gave his name, and after shaking hands, Hall waved him to the armchair beside the desk. Hall tilted his blond head toward the back of the building and said, "I live back there, but I'll bring the bottle in here."

He was gone only a moment and returned with a bottle, a pitcher of water and two glasses. He didn't bother to ask Hanaway how he wanted his drink; he poured a generous amount of whiskey into each glass, gave each a touch of water, then sat down in the swivel chair and faced Hanaway. He lifted his glass and said, "Here's damn all to every banker."

Hanaway lifted his glass and said, "To one especially."

They drank and then Hall said, "Then you know him."

"Only what I saw of him this morning. Heard of him, though, and nothing good. I worked for his uncle up north."

"Didn't know he had one, but then he's got everything else. Why not an uncle?"

"Inherited money?"

Hall nodded. "Lots of it, but it's going down the drain."

"Where?"

Hall looked at him sharply and took a drink. Then he asked quietly, "You an investigator of some sort? For the tame bank stockholders? No, they'd be afraid."

"No." He hesitated, "Well, maybe. But why would the bank stockholders hire an investigator?"

"That story's a long time telling."

Hanaway said, "I've got plenty of it if you have."

Hall nodded. "All right. It begins with a girl, a really beautiful one, named Anne Reeves. She's got a good-for-nothing older brother, name of Dave. To get at the girl, Ben has to buy his way past Dave. Ben's made him consulting geologist for Consolidated Kittrick Gold, and he couldn't tell marbles from chalk, let alone gold." Hall drank again.

After brief reflection, Hanaway asked, "Wouldn't it be cheaper for Ben to marry this Anna?"

Hall smiled wrily, "Have you seen the Kittrick house?"

"Yes, I was in it earlier."

"Well, on the second floor back of that house is Mrs. Ben Kittrick. She comes out on the street about twice a year."

"Crazy?"

"Ben hasn't found a doctor he can pay to say so. She's just mean and vengeful enough so she won't turn Ben free, not even for a lot of money."

Hanaway thought a moment, sipping his drink. Finally he asked, "Is the bank sound? Is the mine sound?"

Hall frowned. "Technically, I'd guess you could say that both are. But here's what's happening. When old George Kittrick founded the town, he built a bank, store, hotel and feed stable with the money from his mine. He would never sell any townsites or land. The bank holds all the paper and the family owns by far the majority of the bank stock." He gestured around him, "He's selling this out from under me, and legally. I haven't the money to buy it, but someone else will have."

This explained a part of Carrie's letter to Uncle Jeff. Ben was looting the estate through the bank. Thinking of Reeves, he asked, "About the Reeveses. Do they throw money around?"

"Dave gambles a lot, but he invests, too. They live well."

He was interrupted by a firm pounding on the door. "It's open," he called.

A blocky man of possibly thirty stepped in, nodded curtly to Hall and laid a cold glance on Hanaway. His eyes were of the palest amber and he couldn't have hid the wildness in them if he'd tried, which he didn't. There was a star pinned to his shirt.

"Hello, Canning," Hall said without much enthusiasm.

"Can I talk to you in private?" the sheriff ignored his greeting.

"No. Can't you see I'm busy with a client?"

"All right. Then your client can hear it too. Ben wants you out of here by dark."

"Me or my possessions?" Hall asked coldly.

"Both." Canning reached in his shirt pocket, pulled out a piece of paper and extended it to Hall. "This here's an eviction notice, all legal-like as you'll see."

"But I won't see," Hall said calmly. "I know what

the form says and I don't intend to read it." He made no move to accept the paper. "Ben gave me a week. You know it, I know, so does Hanaway here. He heard it. Right, Hanaway?" Hanaway nodded.

"Take it!" Canning ordered. When Hall made no move, the sheriff advanced a half step. "Do I have to make you take it?"

"Yes, you do. How, I don't know. You're not carrying a warrant."

Canning's glance had already taken in the whiskey bottle and water pitcher on Hall's desk. He said now, "You drunk or something?"

"I'm not drunk, but maybe something. I'll be checking in at the hotel by dark. The office door key will be at the hotel. If Ben wants the office and my living quarters empty by dark, I think both of you should start rounding up a moving crew. The crew can put everything out in the street. But carefully, please."

For a disbelieving second the sheriff stared at him, and then the wildness in his eyes exploded.

His hand streaked for his gun, but Hanaway dove quickly out of his chair and lunged for the sheriff's right arm. He grabbed it, clamped down, then swung behind the sheriff, put his left arm across the sheriff's throat and bent his head back.

"You damned fool," Hanaway said hotly, quickly. "He hasn't got a gun. But when I let you go, remember that I have."

He swung the sheriff aside and let him go. The sheriff caught his balance, his hand still on his gun. Hanaway watched that hand and when it relaxed looked up into Canning's madman's eyes. "You're kind of jumpy," he observed.

"Who are you?" the sheriff asked in a hard and angry voice.

"Hanaway," Hall said.

"Where from?"

"It doesn't matter," Hanaway said. Curiously, he asked, "What were you going to do if I hadn't jumped you?"

13

"Buffalo him, shove that paper in his pocket and leave," Canning said flatly.

Hanaway looked at Hall and shrugged.

Hall said to the sheriff, "You've served your paper, Wes. Now get the hell out."

The sheriff, still angry, turned and headed for the door. There he halted, turned and said, "I'll be back."

When neither man answered, he went out, leaving the door behind him open. Hall moved over and closed it, then turned to look at Hanaway. "You're in trouble. He's a damned Indian."

"More trouble than you?"

"Hell, I already got some."

III

Ben waited until Sarita had served dessert and returned to the kitchen before he asked, "What's this Steve tells me about some tough cowboy calling here this afternoon?" He looked pleasantly enough at Carrie across the table.

Neva said, "I didn't think he looked tough, Ben."

"Carrie?" Ben asked.

Carrie, about to begin on her dessert, paused and said, "Why, he's done work for Uncle Jeff up north. He was passing through and stopped to say hello." No lies yet, thought Carrie, but there would be more questions.

"Is roughing up Steve just saying hello?"

Carrie looked at him, genuinely surprised. "I didn't know he did. When?"

"Before you were called to the door, Steve said. Who is he? What's his name?"

"Hanaway," she said.

Ben ceased eating, spoon poised over his dish of fruit. "Hanaway? Hal Hanaway, would it be?" At Carrie's tentative nod, Ben said, "He's the bank's newest customer. He opened a drawing account today."

A fleeting anger touched Carrie; when it was gone, she said, "That sounds like he's staying."

"If he is, don't let him in again," Ben said flatly. "I won't have you girls annoyed."

Carrie nodded, watching her brother. He's getting jowls just like Papa's, she thought. He looked altogether like their father, in fact—a florid but handsome man, tall with heavy shoulders, dark straight hair, full black mustache, small hands that had never known labor, and a pleasure in good clothes that was almost feminine.

She finished her dessert while Neva poured their coffee. Ben lit a cigar, tasted his coffee, put down the cup and said, "Queer we haven't heard from Uncle Jeff's lawyer. About his estate, I mean, since we're his only heirs."

"I don't think you'll be hearing from him," Carrie said. "He gave his place to Hanaway."

Ben glared at her, his face flushing with sudden anger.

"Did he say that?"

"Yes, how else would I know?" Carrie said defensively.

Neva said, "Was it much of a ranch, Ben?"

"I don't know, but I'd guess not. Father never thought much of Uncle Jeff's ability to make money. Still, that's not the point. He gave away something that rightfully belongs to us."

"But it was his to give away, wasn't it?" Carrie asked.

"We all know he was sick and old," Ben said slowly. "I wonder if we could prove he wasn't of sound mind when he gave the place to Hanaway."

Both girls watched him in silence, but Carrie was uncomfortable. Apparently Hanaway was going to stay in town. Inevitably Ben would talk with him. After her curt dismissal of Hanaway that afternoon, the man would feel no obligation to her. He just might tell Ben that he was here in answer to a call for help from her. If Ben discovered that, it would enrage him beyond belief. With the dismal feeling that there was real trouble ahead for her, she wished defeatedly that she'd never sent that letter.

Ben finished his coffee, rose and said, "I think I better talk with this fellow."

Carrie rose too, saying, "I think you're wrong, Ben. You think he'd be foolish enough to tell you Uncle Jeff was crazy?"

Ben smiled faintly. "Maybe he won't know he's telling me." Moving toward the door, he said, "I'll be late, so good night."

The two girls said good night. When the sound of

the front door shutting came to them, Neva said, "Why do you always cross Ben, Carrie?"

"Maybe it's because we look at things differently," Carrie answered calmly as she picked up her cup and saucer. "Did Ben ever go up and see Josephine when he got home?"

"Not that I know of."

Carrie shook her head. "He leaves his room in the morning before she's awake. He has his noon meal at the hotel or with one of the Reeveses. He doesn't see her when he gets home, then goes out for the evening. If that's marriage, I'll stay an old maid."

"There you go again," Neva said accusingly.

"Yes, there I go again."

Ben didn't find Hanaway at Brady's crowded saloon, so he headed for the saloon off the lobby of the Kittrick House. This room had some pretensions to elegance. Its paneled walls held prints of famous horses and there was a large card table on either side of the door from the lobby. With its polished walnut bar and scrollwork back bar and mirror, it wasn't the kind of drinking place that would appeal to a rough cowpuncher, Ben guessed as he entered the lobby, but he'd give a look.

A half dozen drinkers were at the bar and there was a card game in progress at one of the tables. Ben looked over the bar drinkers and saw no one resembling the travel-beaten puncher he had only caught a glimpse of in the bank. Then Hanaway turned his head and Ben remembered the profile of the long face.

He went over and joined Hanaway at the bar.

"I'm Ben Kittrick. My sisters said you stopped by the house this afternoon," he said pleasantly and extended a hand.

Hanaway accepted it, saying, "Hal Hanaway here."

"I know. You opened an account at my bank today."

He signaled the bartender and ordered drinks for

them both, then regarded Hanaway with apparent friendliness.

"Carrie said you told her you worked for Uncle Jeff up north."

"Five years," Hanaway said, nodding.

The bartender poured their drinks and moved away. Ben stared after him somberly. "You know, I suppose this happens to a lot of people. They take friends and relatives for granted, like me. Then a death happens, and you wonder why you were so thoughtless, so careless and selfish." He shrugged as he turned again to Hanaway.

"Letters would have been so easy to write. Birthdays aren't hard to remember, either. Still, you kept putting it off—until it's too late. Afterward, you feel like hell."

Hanaway nodded. "That happens to most of us, I reckon."

Ben lifted his drink. "Here's to Uncle Jeff. That's too late too."

They both drank, and Ben once more signaled the bartender, then turned to Hanaway. "Was the end pretty rough for him? We got no details from the woman that worked for him. Just that he died."

"Not too rough. When he got so crippled up he couldn't ride a horse, he just quit."

"Well, he was in his eighties." Ben looked at his new drink. "How was the end? The last letter we got from him said he was going blind. The letter sounded as if going blind might have touched him a little."

"Touched?"

"Well, 'tetched' then. Affected his mind, I mean."

"Not that any of us noticed."

"You couldn't be mistaken on that? His last letter asked about people here that had been dead for years. He assumed we knew people we'd never known. He said Aunt Lucy was well. She's been dead ten years. He asked what he owed on a note. He'd paid it off long ago. Things like that."

Hanaway shook his head in negation. "He was slow-ing up a little toward the end, but he kept his memory."

"Then how do you account for what he wrote?"

"I don't."

"He left you his spread, Carrie said. Why'd he do that?" Ben asked, an aggressiveness in his voice that he didn't try to hide.

"I reckon it was because I took care of him. I was his closest friend and neighbor," Hanaway said easily.

"And you took care to make sure he signed his property over to you."

Hanaway said with vast patience, "No. That was his own idea."

"He had living relatives, but he gave it away to a stranger. That doesn't make sense. You talked him into it."

"You're forgetting one thing," Hanaway said.

"What's the one thing?"

"Why, he didn't like you or your father before you. He figured you had too much money already."

Ben listened politely, then smiled. "Nobody has too much money—except you. I intend to take that ranch from you."

"Like to start trying now?" Hanaway asked quietly.

"I don't think you're carrying the ranch in your hip pocket," Ben said drily.

"What if I was?"

"I might try."

"You'll get the chance. Come along." Hanaway turned and went into the lobby and headed for a writing desk in the back corner. Without sitting down, he took a sheet of paper from the desk rack and, dipping a pen in the glass inkwell, began writing. Finished, he handed the paper to Ben, saying, "There's my deed to the Bar K. Witness it, then give it back. After that, try to take it away from me. It'll be in my hip pocket."

"You're crazy," Ben said.

He took the pen, affixed his signature to the deed, then folded the sheet and was putting it in his pocket when Hanaway hit him. His fist came square on Ben's nose, as was intended.

The immediate pain made Ben lift his hands to his face. Simultaneous with the pain came a flood of tears into his eyes. Hanaway drove his fist into Ben's midriff and watched as Ben's breath exploded from his chest. Ben bent over, dripping blood from his nose, lost his balance and sprawled to the floor.

Stooping, Hanaway reached into Ben's pocket and retrieved the deed. He was straightening up when someone crashed into him and sent him sprawling beyond Ben's body.

Hanaway rolled over to find himself looking up at a man he had never seen before. He was a tall man, red-haired and freckle-faced, dressed in a townsman's suit.

Beside him now, kneeling beside Ben, was a girl in her twenties. Her hair under her small hat was so pale it almost had no color. Her face was dark-skinned and had the flawless perfection of a cameo, but there was alarm and concern in it now.

Hanaway rose and said, "I didn't know you were invited," to the redhead, then added, "Maybe we better take this outside."

"Leave him alone!" the redhead said.

The girl looked at Hanaway, her dark eyes bright with anger. "We both saw you hit him!"

"I always hit a thief," Hanaway said. The elderly clerk came up to them, wringing his hands, and they all watched Ben, on his knees now, reach for his handkerchief and put it to his bloody nose before he came to his feet.

In a muffled voice he said, "Take me to Doc Winters, Anna. My nose feels broken. You go find the sheriff, Dave."

Anna Reeves took Ben by the arm and steered him toward the lobby door; Dave Reeves trailed them, glaring over his shoulder at Hanaway.

When they were gone, Hanaway went back into the bar. The action in the lobby had taken place out of the sight of the saloon patrons who were still drinking. The bartender gave him a close look as Hanaway came up to the bar.

"I think I left a drink."

"That's right. You did. Paid for. Will Mr. Kittrick be back?"

"No." Hanaway got his drink, downed it, said good night to the bartender, crossed the lobby and went out into the night. He crossed the dark street and took up his position in the night-black doorway of an unlighted store.

He'd probably been a damn fool to hit Kittrick, but the arrogance of the man irritated him. Ben's calm assumption that he could claim Jeff's ranch added to the irritation. The warranty deed to the ranch had been drawn up by a lawyer and the signature witnessed by two of Jeff's friends, one a doctor and the other a judge, both of whom could testify to Jeff's sound mind. For a few gray and dismal moments Hanaway wondered if the ranch was worth bucking what he was faced with—two girls who didn't want his help, a powerful and crooked man who, after tonight, would be out to get him; a paranoid sheriff with a hair-trigger temper, and a town that danced to Ben's tune. Then he knew, worth it or not, he would keep his promise to Jeff.

His grim reverie was interrupted by the sight of Sheriff Canning and Dave Reeves climbing the step to the hotel veranda and disappearing into the lobby. It was only moments before a lamp was lighted in his corner room.

He waited. Canning and Reeves waited. Hanaway judged both men were of the same temperament—impatient and easily bored.

In less than five minutes the lamp was extinguished. Moments later Canning and Reeves came out of the hotel and headed downstreet for Brady's.

Once they were past the corner, Hanaway crossed over to the hotel, noiselessly walked through the carpeted lobby, past the clerk doing his bookkeeping, back to the lobby, in the cubbyhole behind the desk, went upstairs and to bed.

21

IV

The first thing Hanaway did after coming down the hotel stairs next morning was to step out onto the veranda and look upstreet at Hall's office. He saw the furniture stacked on the sidewalk, leaving a small passageway for pedestrians. Ben Kittrick had got Hall's message and acted on it.

Turning, Hanaway walked back across the lobby and passed through the open door of the dining room. He spotted Hall at a side table, said good morning and sat down.

"Looked up the street?" Hall asked.

Hanaway nodded. "Anything I can do?"

Hall's waitress came over, gave Hanaway a cup of coffee, took his order and left. When she was gone, Hall said imperturbably, "Yes, but it's not worth the trouble. Legally I'm entitled to five days notice before I can be evicted, but it's only putting it off."

"Where do you go now?"

Hall swallowed a chunk of ham and said, "I scouted around after you left. Found a place Ben has already sold to a saddle maker who's going broke and welcomed the chance to sell it to me on a long-term deal. It's on a side street, but I figure anyone who wants a lawyer besides Ben's, they can find me."

"Need some help moving?"

"Sure. I'll pay you in legal services. I think you'll be needing some."

"Last night? So that's around already."

Hall nodded. "Must have been fun. It would have been for me, anyway."

The waitress came with his breakfast then and Hanaway found that he was almost savagely hungry. Hall was silent, figuring the talk could come later.

Since he was facing the lobby door, he saw the sheriff first and said, "Oh, oh."

When Hanaway looked up at him, Hall said, "Don't look around, but Canning is coming over."

"All right. What's my move?"

"Let me make it."

Canning came up to the table. He paused by Hanaway and did not even look at Hall. "You're under arrest, Hanaway. Come along."

Hall asked mildly, "To where?"

Now the sheriff looked at him. "To jail. But what's it to you?"

"I'm his attorney," Hall retorted. "What's the charge and let's see your warrant."

"Assault and battery. Malicious mischief. Disturbing the peace," Canning replied with obvious pleasure. He took a piece of paper from his hip pocket and handed it to Hall who barely glanced at it.

"What's all this talk about jail? These are all bailable offenses in magistrate's court," Hall said.

"Bailey's out of town and will be for a week. I got to hold him until Bailey gets back."

Hall leaned back in his chair and said drily, "You're getting a little too big for your britches, Wes, but then you always were. These alleged offenses were committed in the City of Kittrick. The arrest should be made by Marshal Barnard, not you."

"The crimes were committed in Kittrick county, and I'm the elected sheriff of that county," Canning said angrily.

"The crimes are misdemeanors, punishable by fines, not prison," Hall said sarcastically. Then he added, "Ben's lawyer out of town too?"

"That's right."

"That's a pity. He could have saved you making a clown of yourself again. You're the wrong man in the wrong place with the wrong warrant, so get away from us. You're spoiling our breakfast."

Canning, just like yesterday, put a hand on his gun and looked at Hanaway, "You coming, Hanaway?"

23

"No, I'm yawning," Hanaway said and continued to eat.

Hall said sharply, "You draw that gun, Canning, and your troubles have just begun. I'll have Hanaway out of jail before you can bring in his dinner. With a writ from Judge Lindsay. I'll also have filed a petition for your recall with the district court." When Canning looked brashly at him, it didn't quite come off; there was doubt in his eyes.

Hall went on with less sharpness in his voice, "Ben's mad and wants to get even. He's ordered you to do something you can't legally do. So Hanaway's free until Ben goes through the proper channels. This is no different than a street brawl between two miners. They're hauled in and fined three dollars apiece. That's what'll happen here. Now goodbye."

Canning's hand fell away from his gun and he took the warrant that Hall extended him. Looking at Hanaway, he said, "I'm not through with you, pilgrim," turned and strutted out of the dining room.

"Got any money?" Hall asked.

"In the bank. Why?"

"When Bailey gets back Marshal Barnard will pick you up and take you before Bailey. I can keep him off your back till then. He's got no love for Canning. Just don't run."

"I'm here for a while," Hanaway said. "What's to do now? Want me to go down to the feed stable and get a team and wagon?"

"All right," Hall said. "I'll go down to Brady's and round up some muscle."

Within a half hour they and two men were hauling Hall's gear into his new office. At the same time, the old tenant, with the help of friends, was moving out. As soon as space was cleared, Hall's furniture went in.

The new building was on the street ending at the Kittrick's house and was roomier than the old one, but with the same arrangment—working quarters in front and, behind a partition, the living quarters. By midafternoon the saddle maker's gear was gone and Hall's possessions were in place. The office, with a window

24

on each side of the street door, looked bare with Hall's few furnishings. It still held the pleasant smell of leather.

Back of the partition there was a bed in a front corner, a deal table with four chairs, stove counter and shelves. Hall was at the stove now, waiting for the pot of coffee to finish its boil. Satisfied that his stove worked well in this new location, he took the pot and moved to the table where Hanaway was seated, two cups on the table before him. Both men were dirty and dusty from sweeping. Hall, his blond hair awry, seemed happy enough with the move. Hanaway, Hall noticed, seemed preoccupied, his long face looking almost doleful.

Hall came over to the table with the coffeepot, filled the two cups, then sat down across from Hanaway. "This morning's session with Canning bothering you?"

"As long as it isn't bothering you, no." Hanaway frowned and went on, "Canning has busted in our talk twice. You never did finish telling me about Reeves."

Hall was silent a while, as if wondering where to begin. Finally he said, "What I'm telling you is only town talk, gossip. A year or so ago Ben Kittrick decided to quit ranching because he's a town boy. The family inherited Diamond K from the old man. It was shipping time, so Ben cleaned out his range. Anything he couldn't sell to these hardscrabble ranchers here, he drove to Junction City and shipped to Kansas City. Two trainloads."

"Breeding stock and all?"

Hall nodded. "Everything. Ben made the trip to Kansas City with the beef. No one commission house for him. He was a smart banker, he figured. He'd let all the commission houses bid on his stuff. He came out good."

He sipped at his coffee, as did the waiting and silent Hanaway.

Hall continued. "On the train back, Ben met Dave and Anna Reeves. Their parents had just died and they were on their way to California to join an older brother. Ben was so taken by Anna's looks that he talked her and her brother into breaking their trip and visiting Kittrick. Diamond K was empty. They could stay there as long as they wanted as his guests. That's how they got here."

Hanaway was still silent, but he was listening very closely, his coffee forgotten.

Hall went on. "I told you Ben gave Dave this job as consultant at Consolidated. Sid Herndon, the super out there, told me Dave gets big money for being totally incompetent. That's Ben's way of paying Anna for her favors."

"Are you telling me what I think you're telling me?"

"That Anna is Ben's mistress? Yes."

Hanaway rose now, a scowl on his face. He walked to the window and gazed unseeing at the vacant lot next door, then turned and made a half circle of the kitchen before he sat down again. He asked, "What's this Anna like?"

"Very pretty, very bright. Some education. Ben introduced us at a horse race they hold a couple of times a year out at the edge of town."

"What about Dave?"

"Shrewd. Good gambler as long as he's sober."

"Did Ben ever check up on them?"

Hall thought a moment. "I don't know. He introduced them as coming from Freeport, Illinois. But why should he check on them? He's not going to marry Anna, because he can't."

Hanaway said quietly, "To find out if they really are brother and sister."

A look of sudden alertness came into Hall's blue eyes. He said, "That's a strange thing to say. What's behind it?"

Hanaway moved his coffee aside, folded his arms on the table and began talking. "I'm only going on what you've told me, so I'll make up a story. Suppose the Reeveses were waiting in Kansas City for a fellow like Ben to show up. Rich and with two trainloads of cattle to make him richer. It wouldn't be hard to find out where he was staying since every commission house would know it. It wouldn't be hard either to find out what train he was leaving on and buy tickets for that train. On the train, Dave would be looking for a card game to kill time. So would Ben. Then Dave introduces Ben to his sister and she takes over. Ben's hooked."

Hall cut in then, smiling. "Comes Ben's invitation to come to Kittrick, since they're footloose anyway. Empty house and all that." He became serious again. "They could still be both crooks and brother and sister."

"I don't think so," Hanaway said stubbornly. "Look what came after. Ben got Anna and paid Dave for her through a job that wasn't a job. You think any brother would sell his beautiful sister to another man? Just the opposite. He'd guard her good name like it was gold and she'd want him to. He'd want to see her marry a good man and raise a family because he's her protector. That is, they'd both feel that way—unless they were trash. And nothing you've said makes them out to be that kind of trash."

Hall looked at him searchingly, rose, and went into his office and came back with a pipe and tobacco pouch. Standing, he packed his pipe, went over to a cupboard and found some matches. Instead of lighting his pipe, however, he moved over to the window, just as Hanaway had done earlier, and put his back to the room.

Presently, he turned and looked at Hanaway. "You know, you've just answered something. I've been asking myself for a year—how Dave could pimp for his sister. The answer is your answer—Anna isn't his sister. They're together in this swindle. This brother-sister business was the only way Dave could cut himself in. If they hadn't claimed that relationship, Ben would have sent Dave packing a year ago."

"Want to prove it?" Hanaway asked.

"Yes. And for the same reason you do, too." He came over and sat down.

27

"Where did you say the Reeveses came from? Freeport, Illinois?"

At Hall's nod, Hanaway said, "All right, you're an attorney settling an estate. Telegraph the sheriff there. Ask for any records of Anna and Dave Reeves's birth. Ask for anything on the parents, or tax records, cemetery records and such. Ask for a reply collect. I'll take your telegram to Junction City and wait for the answer."

"No, you won't. I'll go myself. You can't leave town," Hall said. "Only one trouble, I'm broke."

"You're not so long as I have money," Hanaway said.

"All right. Now tell me why you're interested in this business of the Reeveses who aren't brother and sister."

So Hanaway told Hall about Carrie's letter to Uncle Jeff and his own reason for being here. It was bluntly, to keep Ben from looting the estate and giving it to Dave and Anna.

V

Next morning after breakfast, Hanaway got his dun from the feed stable and began to retrace his route, heading for the bank. Hall was taking the late morning stage to Junction City and Hanaway had to get some money for him.

It was another cloudless day, already beginning to warm up and Hanaway wondered when, if ever, this monotonous hot weather would change. It was too bland for his taste, he decided; he liked the variety and capriciousness of the weather in his own country further north. At least it kept you guessing and this country didn't.

In front of the bank he saw the Kittrick buggy drawn up to the tie rail. Steve was sitting in the driver's seat. Hanaway got no greeting, swung under the tie rail and entered the bank.

There were customers at both windows and Hanaway joined the shortest line. He spent a few moments studying the back of the neck of what must have been a rather pretty woman when he heard the clunk of a heavy door closing. Turning his head, he saw Carrie Kittrick coming toward him from Ben's office. She was hatless, dressed in a short-sleeved, maroon-colored dress and her glance touched him, went beyond him, then abruptly returned to him. She broke her stride, then lifting her chin, regained it and, ignoring him, headed for the door.

Hanaway stepped alongside her, saying, "Morning, Miss Kittrick."

She looked sideways at him, plain anger in her blue eyes, halted and said tartly, "You're not lacking for nerve, are you, Mr. Hanaway?"

29

Hanaway only said, "I was coming to see you this morning."

"You wouldn't have been let in."

Riding over her last word came the angry voice of Ben Kittrick. "Hanaway, take your money out of my bank! And get away from my sister!"

Hanaway turned his head and, along with the other customers, stared at Ben. Even at this distance he could see that Ben's nose was enormously swollen. The skin around both eyes held a purple tinge that gave him the appearance of wearing a mask.

"Later," Hanaway said. He turned now to Carrie and said, "Let's take a walk."

"To where?" she asked coldly.

"I'm going to talk to you. Not in your buggy, either."

"And I will not talk with a bully like you in my buggy or anywhere else," she answered in a low, tight, angry voice.

"I think you will. Stop and think a minute."

She looked at him with hatred and after a moment said, "The letter, you mean."

He nodded. "Ben's right here."

"Where shall we go?" Her tone of voice was resigned.

"What's the matter with the hotel veranda? It was empty a few minutes ago."

"Ben will see us or hear about us," Carrie said bitterly.

"We were talking about your Uncle Jeff. Nobody can prove we weren't."

Wordlessly she turned and left the bank, the towering Hanaway following her. She called to Steve in the buggy, "I'll be back in a little while, Steve." Steve nodded reluctantly.

Side by side, they crossed the street, mounted the two steps to the hotel veranda which held twenty scattered barrel chairs, and sought the far corner.

When Carrie was seated, Hanaway slouched into a chair facing her, took off his stetson and tossed it into an empty chair. They regarded each other in silence

30

which Carrie finally broke, saying, "Why don't you begin?"

"Don't quite know how, but here goes," Hanaway said slowly. "How much do you know about what's going on between Ben and Anna Reeves?"

"Nothing."

"Try again."

"Well, he spends most of his spare time with her."

"Does Ben come home every night?"

"I don't pay any attention."

"Try again," Hanaway said once more.

"He's a grown man!" Carrie said with a flash of anger. "I'm his sister, not his keeper!"

"You've answered my question." He hesitated, then asked, "Do you know her?"

Carrie nodded shortly. "Barely. Ben's not likely to invite her to our house. She isn't likely to invite me to theirs, either."

"Has he moved any clothes out?"

Surprisingly, Carrie flushed. She only nodded her head in the affirmative.

"I don't think Anna and Dave are brother and sister," Hanaway said. "Have you ever thought of that?"

Carrie's lips parted in genuine surprise. She thought a moment before answering, "No, but why did you?"

Hanaway pretty much repeated what he had said about the Reeveses to Hall yesterday, laundering it some, and Carrie listened attentively. When he finished, she nodded thoughtfully. She said in a low voice, "I've thought the whole arrangement was sickening—but I've tried not to think of it."

"Have you talked it over with Neva?"

"Never. Ben can do no wrong for her." She paused, then asked, "How does knowing this change anything?"

"If we can get proof the Reeveses aren't brother and sister, then Ben will boot out Dave," Hanaway answered. "He might boot them both, but I doubt it. Still, with Dave out, you Kittricks will have only

Anna to support. One less than two." He rose now and reached for his hat.

Carrie, still sitting, watched him. "Why are you telling me this?"

It was Hanaway's turn to look surprised, "Why, I'm working for you, like I said I was, like I promised Jeff."

Carrie rose, shaking her head. "You are an exasperating damn man. No, I said that wrong. You are a damned exasperating man."

For the first time they smiled at each other.

VI

On parting with Carrie at the buggy, Hanaway went
into the bank and drew out his money, asking for
double eagles. Ben was nowhere in sight. Afterward
he went back to his room, put the coins in his money
belt and strapped it on under his shirt. He didn't like
to do this, but Ben Kittrick gave him no alternative.
To leave it with a strange hotel owner or saloonkeep-
er—probably Kittrick's men—would be like giving it
away. He also removed a worn envelope from his
bedroll and pocketed it.

When he went downstairs, the stage was pulled up
in front of the hotel. Harry Hall was sitting on one of
the veranda chairs and rose when Hanaway came
over. When Hanaway gave him three double eagles,
Hall shook his head and grinned.

"A real good lawyer would pay his own expenses
and bill you, Hanaway, but rent day always cleans
me out."

"Now or later, what's the difference? How long do
you think you'll take?"

"Three days, I'd reckon. A day for the message to
get there, a day for the sheriff to go over tax records
and check around, and a day for his telegram to
reach me. Maybe it'll be sooner."

The driver came out of the hotel bar then and Hall
picked up his small valise, said half seriously, "Watch
your back trail, friend," and headed for the stage.

Once it had pulled out, Hanaway cut over for his
horse.

VII

That same morning, Dave and Anna Reeves had a late breakfast, as usual. Nobody cared what time Dave showed up at his office at the mine because he did nothing but argue with Sid Herndon, super of the Kittrick Consolidated, as to what drift or crosscut looked promising or was petering out or should be abandoned.

Their breakfast was served by Lupe, a plump little Mexican woman, in the dining room of the big house that Ben Kittrick had turned over to them. As soon as she had poured their second cup of coffee, she went back to the kitchen and closed its door, leaving them free to talk.

Anna spoke first, "I wonder what kind of a day Ben had."

"You don't really care, do you? At least he didn't spend it here." Then he added, "For a change."

Anna smiled. She was wearing a bright red wool wrapper which, when she leaned forward to drink her coffee, revealed that she wore nothing under it. From the cave man on, male mythology has had it that a woman at breakfast isn't really worth looking at. Anna was the exception. Her dark-skinned face was serene as if from fulfillment, her ashen hair neatly braided in a long pigtail, her dark eyes not sleepy but alert and at the same time content. "Oh, Ben's all right. Sometimes I almost like him. At least I don't like to see him get his face smashed in." She frowned slightly at this and said, "I wonder about this Hanaway. Is he trouble for us?"

Dave took a sip of his coffee, put the cup down and regarded it thoughtfully. He was dressed in clean range clothes, but it wouldn't have taken a very sharp

34

observer to know he was in costume. With his sallow, unlined and narrow face under a cap of curly red hair, small uncalloused hands and high, unmuscled shoulders, it was plain he was an indoor man, a city man. His hooded pale eyes held the look of a predatory gambler.

"It's too early to tell yet. I couldn't get much out of Ben." He looked up now. "Ben thinks he conned the Kittrick's uncle out of the old boy's ranch. That started the fight."

"But what's he doing here?" Anna asked.

Dave smiled faintly, "Ben said he's just passing through. I've got another notion, though. The old boy likely told him about the Kittrick money here. And about the two unmarried sisters, neither of them too hard to look at. That would bring him here in a hurry."

Anna smiled too. "We were in line first."

"And that's where we'll stay, Sis."

"You don't have to call me Sis when we're alone, honey," Anna said gently.

"Yes, I do. It's got so I think of it as your real name. If I slip and call you Anna, it doesn't really matter to anyone but me. I just want to hammer home that 'Sis' to everyone, every place. You know that."

Anna sighed. "Yes, you're right."

Dave finished his coffee and rose. Anna rose too. They looked at each other wordlessly, then Dave came to her, arms spread, and Anna moved against him. He hugged her to him and they kissed affectionately.

When they separated, Dave held her shoulders and said, "I'll see Ben first thing. You better go in as soon as you're dressed and see him too. Even if he isn't there again today, we've got to show the colors."

"I was planning to. He'll be feeling so sorry for himself, and that won't do," Anna said, and smiled. She patted his cheek affectionately and he turned away.

Leaving by the living room door, Dave headed for the barn. In the corral adjoining it, José, Lupe's

35

husband, was saddling Dave's horse. Dave halted at the corral gate, leaned against the corral and looked back at the house almost hidden by the tall cottonwoods. It was a big two-story frame affair, built by George Kittrick to house his wife and three children. The servants' quarters were in a low one-story adobe building behind it. According to Ben, when he and his sisters reached school age, their father built another house in town to be nearer school. When both parents died, Ben kept this house and eventually, since he had no interest in ranching, leased the vast range to neighboring cattlemen.

Altogether, Dave thought, he and Anna had lucked out. He'd met Anna two years ago in Chicago where she was waiting tables in the dining room of the hotel where he was living. Her father, a widower, had been a grain speculator, and after a series of disastrous wrong guesses he had shot himself, leaving Anna not only penniless, but without even a home. It was taken by creditors.

Dave had been a successful gambler then and after a short courtship she agreed to live with him, but she would not marry him. She was certain that with her beauty she would attract a rich man, not as a mistress, but as a legal wife. She was close to it with Ben, whose ailing wife would either go crazy or die. It was a lucky night when Dave was caught cheating in a high-stake poker game. They'd had to leave Chicago and head West, and it had been a simple matter to check on Ben Kittrick at his hotel in Kansas City, learn he was rich and arrange to travel on the same train with him. Anna did the rest.

Dave heard José approaching with his horse and opened the gate. Since Dave could speak no Spanish and José no English, they only smiled at each other. Dave mounted, picked up the road and headed across the mile of mesquite and cactus desert that reached to the edge of town. Off to the right and two miles from town, the San Soba mountain, known locally as the Flattops, shouldered a couple of thousand feet off the desert floor; the Kittrick Consolidated Mine and Mill sprawled at its base.

In town, Dave stopped at the bank, dismounted, walked past two lines of customers and knocked on the door of Ben's office. A surly voice said from inside, "Come in," and Dave stepped into the office.

Ben sat in a leather-covered swivel chair behind a massive flat paper-littered desk and Dave, seeing his face, halted abruptly and stared. "Good God. You look like you've been run over by a train, Ben."

"I feel like it and sound like it too. I've got a nose full of cotton," Ben growled. He had been writing and he tossed his pen toward the inkstand. "Forgot to mention it that night, but thanks for helping me with Hanaway. I'm sure he was getting ready to kick me to pieces when you came."

"That's what I figured too," Dave lied. He moved over to a leather-covered easy chair and sank into it. "We tried to see you yesterday, but the girls didn't think you were up to it."

"I wasn't."

"What are you going to do about this fellow, Ben?"

Ben told him of Canning's attempt to arrest Hanaway and of Hall's stopping him. "The magistrate's due back today, but I don't expect much from him. He always sides with the miners against me, so why not a stranger? He'll side with Hanaway."

"Doesn't Canning know some roughs that could take care of him?"

Ben nodded. "We'll wait and see what the marshal and the magistrate do. If they go easy on him, I'll still get a piece of his hide." He leaned back in his chair. "How's Anna?"

"You know Sis. She's worried half crazy about you. She'll be in to see you later."

Ben smiled. "She won't like what she sees."

"No, she won't, but I don't think she likes you only for your beauty," Dave said, half seriously, half jokingly.

Ben laughed and nodded. "I feel that same way about her, only I'm glad she's beautiful."

Dave rose, saying, "Well, our mother saved everything in that line for Sis. She didn't waste any of it on me or my brother."

Again Ben laughed and rose and said, "My mother too. She saved it for the girls." He came around the desk and extended his hand. "I put something in the mail for you today. A little token of thanks for the other night."

Dave shook hands with him, but he was shaking his head in negation. "No, Ben, if it's what I think it is, I'll burn it. You don't reward your friends, you expect them to help you when you need it."

Ben shrugged and said, "Suit yourself, but still my thanks."

Outside Dave allowed himself a smile. Ben's money was always welcome, but not this time. He was certain that if he destroyed this check Ben would add the sum and more to his salary check. Besides, his defense of Ben put Ben in his debt. In a way, that was more important than anything else.

The ride out to the mine was a bore, but necessary. He had to go through the motions of work to justify his monthly check, not that he followed Herndon or even the lowliest miner. No matter how many books on geology he read, he lacked not only interest, but any practical mining experience. The only two people he had deceived were Carrie and Neva and that was only because they weren't even curious and were too rich to care.

The tall headframe of the Consolidated and the smoking smelter stacks loomed up a half mile ahead, silhouetted against the eroded dust-colored face of the Flattops. Closer, other buildings—the machine shop, cook shack, pump house, the long adobe dormitories and the company store—could be made out. For six and a half days these miners worked in this womanless world.

Dave headed directly for the open-faced shed and corral near the adobe office building. He tied his horse in the shed, slipped the bit and loosened the cinch, then tramped across the hard-packed earth toward the office building. A horse stood hipshot at the tie rail, he noted.

He did not head for the main office entrance beyond the tie. Instead, he walked toward the door at the far corner. This originally had been a storeroom which had been cleaned out and whitewashed to make an office for him.

Unlocking the door, Dave swung it open, took a step inside, then halted abruptly. Hanaway was seated in the chair alongside a roll-top desk, hat on his legs.

Dave closed the door, leaned against it and said harshly, "What in hell are you doing in my office?"

Hanaway nodded to the open door that led into the large room holding several desks behind a low railing. "They told me to wait in here."

"Get out!" Dave said sharply.

Hanaway asked mildly, "You treat the rest of Consolidated stockholders like this?"

Reeves stared angrily at him. "You a Consolidated stockholder? That's a laugh. All stock is family-held, so your bluff won't work. Now get out before I call someone in to throw you out!"

Hanaway smiled thinly and rose. "I notice you didn't say before I throw you out!" He reached in his hip pocket for an envelope, drew a sheaf of papers from it, unfolded and extended them, saying, "Be very careful to return them unless you like what Ben got."

Dave moved over and took the papers. They were Consolidated stock certificates; he studied them carefully. "Why, these are made out to Jeff Kittrick, not to you."

"Look on the back. He signed them over to me before he died."

Reeves turned them over. "Four of them for twenty-five shares each." He looked up. "I'll keep these to show Ben. I think you forged the old boy's signature, but Ben'll know."

"You weren't listening," Hanaway said quietly.

Reeves folded the certificates and put them in his shirt pocket. "You'll get them back."

"I'm sure I will," Hanaway murmured. He held out his hand and added, "Right now."

"After they're checked by . . ."

Hanaway had started to draw back his hand, then took a step quartering to Dave's right. His arm traveled less than twenty inches to Reeves's solar plexus. Dave's breath exploded out of his cheeks in a grunting bray, and he fell backward, knees drawn to chest. Almost slowly, Hanaway moved in, retrieved the certificates, pocketed them and then went back to the chair he had just vacated.

Someone in the outer office, an elderly heavy-set man, stepped into the room through the connecting door. He was in his shirtsleeves, his vest unbuttoned, a pencil behind his ear. He looked through iron-rimmed glasses at Reeves, whose legs were slowly straightening out, then he looked at Hanaway.

"What happened?"

"He ever had these fits before?" Hanaway asked.

"Not that I know of."

"I've heard they ought to be left alone, then they come out of it. Me, I wouldn't like to get bit by him."

"Yes," the old man agreed uncertainly. Then he made up his mind, turned and went back to the big office.

Hanaway watched Reeves. His eyes opened and he stared at the ceiling for long moments, then slowly pushed himself to a sitting position. He saw Hanaway and gave him a look of purest hatred.

"You like it down there or do you want to sit down at your desk and talk?"

Reeves didn't answer, only came slowly to his feet, took three uncertain steps to his desk swivel chair and slacked into it. "What is it you want?" he asked in an uncertain voice.

"A look at your payroll books. That's my right as a stockholder."

Reeves slowly shook his head. "I've got no authority to show them to you. I've never seen them myself."

"But you're not a stockholder and I am."

Reeves was still shaking his head. "You'll have to go

through Ben. Unless you pull that gun and hold up everybody in the office."

"Not a bad idea. Show me the way. Take me to the company treasurer."

Reeves rose unsteadily. "That would be Miss Neva Kittrick. All officers are Kittricks. Only Ben works at it."

"Head bookkeeper then. You do the talking."

Hanaway waited, watching Reeves, whose glance now fell away. Reeves moved past him and entered the big room, Hanaway behind him. A low railing with a swing gate opposite the outside door ran the length of the room, which held four regular desks and a high bookkeeping desk against the rear wall. The vault door to one side of this desk was open and seated on a high stool was the old man who had seen Reeves on the floor. Two of the other desks were occupied by middle-aged men in shirtsleeves whose coats were draped over the backs of their chairs.

Reeves walked up to the old man on the high stool and halted beside him. "Walters, this is Hal Hanaway, a Consolidated stockholder."

"You all right now, Mr. Reeves?" When Reeves nodded curtly, Walters looked at Hanaway with cautious curiosity. "A stockholder, you say? I don't see how that can be."

Hanaway produced the certificates and handed them to Walters. The old man looked immediately on the reverse side of the certificates and murmured, "A transfer from old Jeff. Well, well. Mr. Hanaway, you own the only Consolidated stock outside the Kittrick family."

"Do I have equal rights with the family?"

Walters nodded promptly. "Yes. The corporation charter was drawn up very carefully. Old Mr. Kittrick wanted it family-owned, each child receiving an equal number of shares. The hundred shares he held out for his brother Jeff was just a brag. He wanted to show his out-of-the-pants cowboy brother that he was a success. But old Jeff never cashed a dividend check.

It backfired on Mr. Kittrick and made him sore, but he couldn't do anything about it."

Hanaway waited him out, then said, "Then I can look at the books?"

"Certainly. What books do you want to look at?"

"You look for me, Mr. Walters." He shifted his glance to Reeves and said, "I want to know how much your consulting geologist has been paid since he was hired."

Walters said almost with relish, "That would be Mr. Reeves." He rose and went into the vault, lighted the lamp, took down a ledger from a shelf and put it on the table by the lamp.

Reeves said drily, "You just got a man fired."

"You, I hope," Hanaway replied.

While Walters was looking up the figures, Hanaway moved to the other side of the desk and looked at the framed photographs on the wall. They began with the original Kittrick mine, nothing more than a tunnel into the Flattops. Progressively, they showed how the Kittrick blossomed into the Consolidated it was to-day. He got only a glimpse of the last photograph when Walters came out of the vault, a folded piece of paper in his hand.

When Hanaway moved over to him and accepted the paper, Walters said, "I'm a fast adder, sir, but I think you'll find the sum correct."

Hanaway put the folded sheet in his pocket, held out his hand and said, "Thank you, Mr. Walters. Sorry I took up your time."

"You have a right to," Walters said, shaking hands with him.

Hanaway looked at Reeves and said, "And thanks to you too, Mr. Reeves. I'll be sure to tell Ben how cooperative you've been."

Reeves looked at him disdainfully. "If you can get close enough to him to talk."

Hanaway went through the swing gate, out the door and mounted his dun. When he was well on his way to town, he took out the paper Walters had given him and unfolded it. It was headed: "Paid to David

42

Reeves." He looked first at the total sum. It amounted to $56,800.00 for thirteen months. Scanning the monthly payments, he noted that they varied widely with seemingly no standard salary. And they of course did not include what Ben had probably paid Reeves out of his own account. Or the cost of Ben's undoubted personal gifts to Anna.

As he pocketed the sheet Walters had given him, he thought, no wonder Carrie wrote Uncle Jeff for a lawyer.

VIII

Harry Hall had finished his supper in the dining room of the Junction City Hotel and gone up to his room. He had sent the telegram last evening and spent the long day drawing up two lengthy contracts for a client and intended to finish them tonight.

He had barely started work when a knock came on the frame of his open door. Looking up from the washstand he was using as a table, he saw a boy standing in the doorway and called, "Come in, son."

The boy, dirty and wearing the shabbiest of clothes, took off his cap, drew an envelope from it and walked across the room, saying, "Mr. Eberle at the depot said to give you this." He put his hand in his pocket and drew out some coins. "You got this comin' too." He put the coins along with the telegram on the tablet Hall had been writing on.

Hall gave him fifty cents and said, "When does the Kittrick stage leave tomorrow?"

"First light, sir."

Hall thanked him and the boy ran out of the room, stammering his thanks over his shoulder. Grateful that the promptness of the telegram had saved him a second day of waiting, Hall tore open the sealed envelope. The message read:

All sources you asked about were checked. No Reeves ever on tax roll or birth records. No Reeves in cemeteries either. No Reeves with an A either. Your money, so good luck.

JOHN A. POE, SHERIFF
Stephenson County,
Freeport, Illinois

Hall felt a surge of elation. Hanaway's hunch had been a good one. The message didn't prove that Anna and

44

Dave Reeves were not brother and sister; it did prove, however, that they had collaborated on a lie about where they'd come from.

Hall finished his second contract, went down to the hotel bar for a nightcap, then went upstairs to bed after leaving a call at the desk to be wakened before stage time.

Arriving in Kittrick in midmorning, Hall dropped off his valise at his office, went upstreet to Charlie Ching's cafe, ate breakfast, then cut over to the hotel. Hanaway was out and Hall left a note for him to come over to see him.

Entering his office, he saw the slim figure of City Marshal Barnard sitting in the chair beside his desk. Barnard rose and they shook hands. The marshal was close to seventy, thin and tall with a full mustache as white as his thick hair and eyebrows over a knife of a Roman nose. He was a gentle man who seldom carried a gun, but in a brawl he was rougher than a strong twenty-year-old.

"Heard you came in on the stage. Thought I'd drop by."

"I know why, too," Hall said. He gestured to the chair and the marshal sat down as Hall swung the swivel chair around and seated himself.

"Where is this Hanaway?" the marshal asked.

"I'm looking for him too, but he's around."

"I know. He ain't checked out of his room. Canning makes damn sure of that every morning early."

Hall smiled. "Those two have got a thing going, I'd guess."

"You don't have to guess. What about this Hanaway and Ben?"

Hall told him what he knew about the brawl in the hotel lobby, and of Canning's attempt to arrest Hanaway.

The marshal only nodded and said in a mild voice, "Then you ain't heard about yesterday?" When Hall said he hadn't, the marshal went on, "He showed up at the Consolidated office with some shares of stock that Jeff Kittrick had signed over to him. Wanted to

45

look at the company books. Dave Reeves said he couldn't, so this Hanaway belted him and got his look at the books, too."

"If he's a stockholder, he has a right to look at the books. I didn't know about his stock, though."

"Ben reckons he's a troublemaker. Do you?"

"Anything but. Ben's used to leaning on people. Hanaway won't be leaned on, is all." Then he added, "Like you."

A slight lift of the marshal's white mustache indicated a smile. He put his hands on the arms of the chair, beginning to rise, when a knock on the door halted him. The door opened and Hanaway stepped inside.

Both Hall and the marshal rose at his entrance and Hall said, "You've got both of us looking for you, Hanaway." As Hanaway came toward them, Hall said, "This is Marshal Barnard, Hanaway. He's our town lawman."

Hanaway and the marshal liked each other on sight as they shook hands. Hanaway was taller by two inches, but the hand he shook was as big and work-worn as his own.

"I was plenty sure I'd meet you, Marshal," Hanaway said. "Matter of fact, the sheriff wanted me to stay with him until you got back."

The marshal nodded. "We'll get done with it at four tomorrow afternoon at the courthouse." He paused and Hall was about to speak when Barnard observed, "You sure changed Ben's face. He kinda looks like a raccoon."

Hall said quietly, "At heart, he is one."

The marshal looked at him and said in a dry tone of voice, "Oh, they're a nice animal. They night-prowl and steal, but they ain't dangerous."

Hall and Hanaway both laughed. The marshal's blue eyes held a quick mischief but he didn't smile. He said mildly, "I'll be seeing you later."

When he had gone, Hanaway said, "He'll do to ride the river with."

"Well, he's not Ben's man, for sure."

"How come you're a day early?" Hanaway asked.

Hall reached in his breast pocket and pulled out the telegram and gave it to Hanaway saying, "It's like they were waiting for me to ask."

Hanaway took out the message and read it. He smiled and handed it back, then slacked into the chair the marshal had just vacated. From his shirt pocket he took out a folded piece of paper and tossed it on Hall's desk. "Fair trade," he said. "That's what Ben has paid Reeves in Consolidated's money."

Hall sat down, read the figures, whistled softly and looked thoughtfully at Hanaway. "I'd guess that's a lot more than Ben took out for the girls and himself and the hired hands."

Hanaway nodded. "Where'd it go? Cards?"

Hall shook his head. "Reeves is a good poker player when he's sober. He's dropped some, but the word is that it's under five thousand." He grinned wryly. "That's a couple of years' fees for me, but it doesn't even dent what he got from Consolidated."

"What's our move, Harry?" Hanaway asked. "I've got my ideas, but give me yours."

Hall tilted his chair back, made a steeple of his hands, put his chin on it and frowned. "When you give that telegram to Ben, he'll blow his stack. He'll . . ."

"When *you* give it to him," Hanaway interrupted, and went on, "remember, I'm a Consolidated stockholder and you're my lawyer."

Hall smiled. "You held that out on me. Why?"

"I don't reckon you'd have let me have my session with Reeves over there at Consolidated. You'd have gone to court for a writ or something, wouldn't you?"

Hall nodded promptly. "I would because it's your legal right to look at the books. But that's water under the bridge. Want me to go on?" At Hanaway's nod, Hall said, "All right, I charge at Ben in your name." He spread his arms now in a gesture of helplessness. "He'll laugh. I'll demand a vote of stockholders. Then comes the second laugh. I'll demand that all money

47

paid Reeves must come out of his shares. Then comes the last laugh. We're nowhere."

Hanaway nodded. "That's the way it should go—except for one thing. Carrie should show him the telegram, with Neva, you and me watching. Then you take over."

IX

"Two men to see you, Miss Carrie."

Carrie, writing a letter at the desk in the library, looked over at Sarita standing in the doorway. "Who are they?"

"One, he's been here, a *caballero*. The other, I don't know."

The *caballero* would be Hanaway, Carrie thought. She rose, saying, "Show them out to the patio where it's cooler. Tell them I'll join them there. Then bring some iced tea out for us."

Sarita left and Carrie went down the hall to her bedroom where she adjusted her tawny hair and smoothed out the skirt of her gray flower-print dress. Since her last talk with Hanaway, she had expected that, in his self-appointed role as her protector, he would keep in touch with her. Her feelings toward him were mixed, a combination of amusement, irritation and, strangely, anticipation.

The side door of her bedroom opened onto the flagstone patio that was shaded by a huge cottonwood tree. As she stepped out the door, Hanaway and his companion rose from burlap-covered slat chairs. Both men had put their hats on the flagstone beside their chairs.

When Carrie approached, she said, "I thought it would be cooler out here. The house is an oven."

Hanaway nodded and said, "Carrie, this is Harry Hall, the lawyer. He says he knows you from a distance, but you've never met."

"And I know him only from a distance," Carrie said and smiled, extending her hand to Hall. "I've heard of you through Ben and Mr. Kelso. He's our lawyer."

49

"Then you haven't heard much good about me," Hall said and he smiled.

Carrie next extended her hand to Hanaway who took it gently as she said to them both, "Won't you sit down."

As they were seating themselves, Sarita came around the kitchen corner of the house with a tray which she placed on the low table.

Carrie said to Hanaway as Sarita left them, "You and Mr. Hall take the two dark ones. There's rum in them. That's Ben's house rule for men's iced tea. He says it's the only way a man can gag it down."

They tasted their drinks and Hall said, "I wish I'd heard about this sooner. You can't taste the tea at all."

Carrie laughed and she looked at Hall appraisingly. "Are you the mining lawyer Uncle Jeff was going to send me?"

Before Hall could answer, Hanaway said, "He's the one and he's already at work." He took some papers from his hip pocket and laid them on the table beside Carrie's glass. "Come to think of it, maybe you should take my drink, Carrie."

Carrie searched his dark and sober face that somehow suggested loneliness and an almost fierce independence. "Meaning those papers you just put down aren't exactly good news?"

"In the long run yes, but not right away," Hanaway said. "Before you read the top one, can you tell me where Dave and Anna Reeves came from—where they grew up?"

Carrie said promptly, "Why, according to Ben, it was Freeport in Illinois."

"Read it," Hanaway said gently.

Carrie picked up the envelope and took out the telegram. After reading it, she reread it, then looked up and beyond Hanaway for a brief moment before returning her glance to him.

"I see," she said softly.

"Now the other," Hanaway said.

Carrie picked up Walter's list and scanned it, then

50

frowned and looked up at Hanaway. "They're amounts, but what do they mean?"

"The sum is what Dave Reeves has been paid by Consolidated," Hanaway said.

"Oh no!" Carrie whispered. She looked at Hall. "Are they true?"

"Hanaway got them from Walters, the bookkeeper at Consolidated," Hall replied.

Carrie's shocked glance shifted to Hanaway. "How did you?"

Hall answered for Hanaway, telling her of the Consolidated shares transferred from Uncle Jeff to Hanaway, and of the scuffle with Reeves before Walters properly gave Hanaway the figures he wanted. Hall went further. "Hanaway said you wrote Uncle Jeff saying Ben was liquidating property and reinvesting the money from them. It's anybody's guess, but mine is that through Consolidated's payroll, he was reinvesting in Dave and Anna Reeves."

Carrie was silent for a long half minute. Neither man spoke, only watched her. Finally Carrie said, "Then the Reeveses are not brother and sister but a pair of swindlers after Ben's money."

"Your money and Neva's money, too," Hanaway said.

Only now did anger come to Carrie. In his supreme arrogance, Ben had never consulted her or Neva, believing as he did that financial affairs were not a woman's business. Only through gossip and guarded questions put to her by women friends had she learned enough of Ben's disposal of their property to write Uncle Jeff asking his help. As vice president of Consolidated and member of the board of directors, she had signed anything Ben told her to sign. The amount of Dave Reeves's salary had surely been hidden in the semiannual report under the heading of Costs of Geological Exploration, always a substantial item over the years. Since the costs were never broken down, she and Neva had never questioned them except once earlier this year. Ben had a perfectly reasonable answer. "We're always exploring, chasing down anything that looks promising. We put on a hunting gang one week, another gang the next. If we stay in business, we've got to find new ore to mine. Sometimes it pans out, but mostly it doesn't, but we have to do it." Yes, exploration costs hid the money Ben paid Dave.

"What should I do about this?" Carrie asked Hanaway. "I'm vice president of Consolidated."

"Ask my lawyer," Hanaway answered, nodding toward Hall.

Hall said, "You're vice president of Consolidated so you can ask about the money paid Dave Reeves. Then show Ben the telegram. If the Reeveses are lying about their birthplace, they could be lying about their relationship."

"I'm sure of that last," Carrie said flatly. The idea of confronting Ben was appalling, but it had to be done.

"As a stockholder in Consolidated, I've got a right to be in on this too. I have a right to bring a lawyer." Hanaway paused and Carrie knew what was coming and her heart leaped.

Hanaway said, "Why don't the three of us tackle Ben?"

X

Ben looked up from the note he held in his hand to regard their white-shirted houseman, Steve.

"What the devil is this?" he asked angrily.

"I don't know, Mr. Ben. Miss Carrie said to give it to you and take you to the place where I let her off."

"And where is that?"

"Across the street and up a ways. Her and Miss Neva went inside."

Ben glanced again at the note which said:

Ben, will you please come now to where Steve shows you.
CARRIE

Ben rose, wadded up the note, rammed it in his shirt pocket and, not bothering to put on his coat, left the bank office, Steve trailing him. His nose had lost its swelling, and the skin around his eyes had turned from purple to a blue-green-yellow. Out on the boardwalk he halted and Steve came up beside him. "Point it out."

"The buggy's right in front of it."

Ben frowned. Hadn't he heard that Harry Hall had moved into one of those store buildings over there? But what business would the girls have with that shyster, he wondered angrily. He started diagonally across the dusty street. He was on a collision course with a delivery wagon but he bulled on. Its driver, seeing this was Ben Kittrick he was about to run down, reined up and let both men pass.

"Right there," Steve said, pointing to a door whose peeling paint announced Tom's Saddlery.

Without bothering to knock, Ben opened the door, took a step inside and halted abruptly. Neva and

53

Carrie, both in white summer dresses, sat in the two leather chairs. Hall and Hanaway rose from kitchen chairs. Hall pointed to another kitchen chair beside Neva's and said, "Morning, Ben. Take a chair."

"Why should I?" To the girls he said roughly, "What are you doing here, you two?"

"Carrie told me to come with her. I don't know why," Neva answered. "Sit down, Ben, and we'll find out."

Ben turned his head slightly to regard Hall and Hanaway with open contempt. Coming slowly forward, he said, "I'm beginning to guess what this is all about."

"I thought you would, but let's get it out in the open. Hanaway here . . ."

"Owns a hundred shares of Consolidated," Ben cut in coldly. "He had a right to look at the books. If he didn't, he'd be in jail right now. What else?"

Reaching in his coat pocket, Hall said, "You'll want a look at the certificates, I guess."

"No," Ben said flatly. "Hanaway tricked Uncle Jeff out of everything he owned. Why not the certificates too?"

Hanaway only smiled. It was a smug smile, purposely so.

"Is that all?" Ben asked brusquely. "I've got work to do."

"No, it isn't all, Ben," Carrie said quietly. "Do you know how much we've paid out to Dave Reeves?"

"Yes. His salary, a good one. Consulting geologists don't come cheap."

Carrie took Walter's list from her purse and unfolded it. She did not rise and go over to Ben, only held it out and waited for him to come over to her. Ben approached her and roughly whipped the paper from her hand. He looked at the figures and his face flushed with anger and embarrassment.

"Let Neva see. It's partly her money," Carrie said.

Ben handed the sheet to Neva, who studied it briefly, started to hand it back, then looked at it again. Looking up at Ben, she said shrewdly, "That's ten times what we pay Sid Herndon, and he runs the mine, Ben." She handed the paper back to Ben who took it angrily.

"I run the mine, not you girls or Herndon!" Ben said roughly. "If I say he's worth it, he is. And I like money better than any of you." He looked at each girl separately. Neva's glance slid away. Carrie's held his until she stared him down.

Ben said sullenly, "This could have been discussed between us, not in front of a broke lawyer and a slick thief." He looked at Hall now. "One hundred shares against sixty thousand. Tell your client to think it over before he starts trouble."

He turned and took a step toward the door when Carrie said in a tone of voice that held a new authority, "Don't go yet, Ben. There's something else."

Ben halted, turned and looked sternly at her. "Which we can talk over privately."

"No. You'll need to question Mr. Hall and Mr. Hanaway in the long run, so why not do it now?" Before he could refuse, Carrie asked, "Where did Dave Reeves come from? The same place as Anna?"

Ben frowned. "That's a silly question, and you know it. They were born seven years apart and raised in Freeport, Illinois. I've told you that."

Carrie again reached into her handbag and brought out the telegram which she extended to Ben who came back to accept it. He read it twice, then looked at Hall. "This is addressed to you. Was it your idea?" His fury almost choked him.

"Mine," Hanaway said. "As a Consolidated stockholder, I was curious what Reeves was paid. Also who Reeves was. So I asked Hall to start at the beginning—Freeport, Illinois."

"You meddling bastard! Stay out of my business!"

"No, I'm just starting," Hanaway said evenly. "Before I'm done, I'll prove the Reeveses are a pair of swindlers that aren't even related."

Ben lunged for him, but Hall stepped in between them, grasped Ben's forearms and wrestled him to a halt. Both the girls had come to their feet. There was dismay in Carrie's face and plain fright in Neva's.

"I'll kill you for this!" Ben shouted.

"Because you know you've been taken?" Hanaway asked, still quietly, and added, "Make sense, man."

Ben wrenched free of Hall, but instead of heading for Hanaway, he turned and strode for the door, yanked it open and crashed it shut.

The men looked at the two girls, observing the effect Ben's raging exit had upon them. Hanaway watched Neva, since she was the sister who thought Ben could do no wrong. Still pale from fright, she asked, "What was it Ben read that made him so mad?"

Hanaway moved over and picked up the salary list and the telegram Ben had dropped and took the telegram over to Neva. She read it carefully and a look of disbelief came to her pretty face as she grasped its significance. She handed the telegram back and looked at Carrie and said accusingly, "You didn't tell me about this either, Carrie."

"You'd only have told Ben about it," Carrie said calmly. "I wanted to surprise you both."

"What will Ben do about it?" Neva asked, indicating the telegram.

"Maybe he'll tell you, but he'll never tell me. Not after today," Carrie said.

XI

When Ben got back to his office, he locked both doors. Sitting down behind his desk, he pulled out a lower drawer, lifted out a bottle of whiskey and a glass, half filled the glass with a shaking hand and drank off the whiskey.

His mind was in such furious turmoil he could not think, could only feel as if he had been gutted. He couldn't doubt the telegram; through bank business he had learned to recognize the Junction City station agent's handwriting. Nor could he doubt the contents of the telegram. Dave and Anna had lied to him about their birthplace. They had lied about the death of their parents as the check of cemetery proved. Had they lied about being brother and sister, as that damned Hanaway had hinted?

But the real, soul-wrenching question Ben asked himself was—had Anna lied when she said she loved him?

Ben groaned aloud and shook his head in negation, as if physically denying even the thought. He knew she loved him as he loved her—entirely, body, soul, and spirit. He could not imagine life without her. If, as that damned Hanaway hinted, Dave and Anna were swindlers, that didn't include Anna. When he had sworn to her that someday they could and would be married, she gave herself to him. She even offered to bear his children out of wedlock until they could be legitimized. Was that the offer of an unloving woman? No. Anna was his as he was hers.

Certain of that, he drank again. Afterward, his nerves quieted, the knot of pain eased, he turned his thoughts to Dave. If there was a swindle involved here, as that damned Hanaway believed, it was

Dave's. Ben had given Dave his fake job only to provide Anna with money to live decently. If Dave and Anna were not brother and sister, then he could get rid of Dave easily by giving Anna enough for her but not enough for Dave too. He would run Dave out of town.

Slowly Ben came to the realization that he was accepting as truth everything that Hanaway had but barely proven, or claimed he could prove in the future. While fighting it and hating it, he more than half believed it, and that position was intolerable. He must take the evidence Hanaway dug up and Hanaway's suspicions and prove them right or wrong himself. Today was as good a time as any to start and he thought he knew how to do it. Anna was coming to town this morning to shop for food and supplies. On these shopping days she and Ben always had dinner together in the suite at the hotel that Ben leased for business meetings requiring privacy. Dave never bothered to ride in and join them, so they would be alone.

Ben put away the bottle of whiskey and glass, unlocked the doors, went out to the vault for some mortgage papers, returned and set about his routine work, fighting his impatience.

Noon found him in the hotel saloon. Drink in hand, he positioned himself so he could watch the lobby in the back-bar mirror. At Anna's entrance, he finished his drink and went out to meet her.

As always, she was stunningly dressed, today in a white basque, the maroon-colored skirt matched by a narrow band on the straw boater pinned atop her pale hair. They shook hands formally as they always did in public, then Ben walked over and spoke briefly to the headwaitress standing inside the open double doors of the dining room. Rejoining Anna, Ben took her arm and they disappeared up the stairway.

The two corner rooms on the south side of the hotel and fronting the street opened on Ben's suite. He unlocked the far door which opened onto a parlor, stepped aside for Anna to pass, went in, closed the door and took her into his arms and tenderly kissed her.

Afterward Anna took off her hat, tossed it on the sofa, then moved over to Ben and kissed him again. There was a round table in the corner by the double doors with a cloth holding two place settings, chairs facing them, just as there was every Wednesday.

Anna went over to a mirror beyond the sofa and was adjusting her hair as Ben asked, "Any surprises in the stores?"

Anna laughed. "Is there ever? I did order a new hat, though. Out of boredom, maybe. Buying groceries doesn't exactly thrill me."

"Why should it? That's for women with ten kids, not for a princess."

Anna turned and threw him a kiss, then came over to the sofa and sat down. "I saw the most beautiful black horse today. His coat was so shiny he was almost blinding in the sun."

"Whose? Where'd you see him?"

Anna smiled. "He wasn't black and I won't tell you where I saw him. You'd only want to buy him for me."

"Certainly."

"You spend too much money on me, Ben. One of the nicest things in life is to want something you don't deserve and know you'll never get."

"Nonsense," Ben growled. He came over and sat beside her, taking her hand and holding it in his.

"What did you do today except loan money at twelve per cent interest?" Anna asked, mischief in her voice.

Ben laughed. "Signed a raft of papers." This was the opening he'd been waiting for and he proceeded in a casual tone of voice. "You know, it helps to have a county and town named after your father. I'd have spent all morning at the courthouse signing stuff to be notarized if my name wasn't Kittrick. Instead the county clerk came to my office because he's clerk of Kittrick County."

"Maybe he likes doing you favors," Anna said.

Ben shrugged. "Funny how counties get their names here in the West. The county east of Kittrick is San Isbel, the county west of us is Rio Blanco. Was it that crazy back east in Illinois? Did they name counties after men and the color of a river and a saint?"

"Freeport is in Coxwell County, named after J. B. Coxwell, a pioneer," Anna said promptly.

Ben only nodded. Remembering the telegram from the sheriff in Freeport, Ben recalled the county was Stephenson. You're lying honey, he thought sadly.

A knock came on the door and Ben rose. This would be a waitress with their dinner.

XII

Hanaway, accompanied by Hall, arrived at the small two-story gray stone courthouse a little after four o'clock that afternoon. It was a block behind the hotel and fairly new, and Hanaway guessed that some old adobe buildings had been razed to make way for it, since the cottonwoods shading it were mature and taller than the building.

In the second-floor courtroom, used by both town and county, there were a dozen people gathered in the seats closest to the rail which separated the jury box, the raised bench and the attorneys' tables from the spectators.

Sheriff Canning was one of the spectators, and beside him sat Dave Reeves. Neither seemed to notice Hanaway as he and Hall took the nearest seats.

The magistrate, a bald man wearing steel-rimmed spectacles, was leaning across the bench listening to Marshal Barnard whose thick hair was an almost blinding white. Standing beside him was a short man in rough working clothes. The magistrate said something to this man who reached in his pocket, put a coin in front of the magistrate, put on a wool hat, came through the swing gate and left.

Marshal Barnard was scanning the courtroom, and when he saw Hall and Hanaway, he beckoned to them. Hall led the way through the gate and he and Hanaway halted before the magistrate, who nodded to them and said, "Hello, Harry." He regarded Marshal Barnard, asking, "What's the man charged with, Marshal?"

"Disturbing the peace. He took a poke at a fellow in the hotel lobby the other night."

The magistrate nodded and said to Hanaway, "How do you plead?"

Hall said promptly, "He pleads guilty, your Honor."

"Well, it'll cost him five dollars for not taking his fight out to the street," the magistrate said.

As Hanaway put a five dollar gold piece before the magistrate, he suppressed a smile. No mention of Ben Kittrick's name, although Hanaway was sure the whole town, including the magistrate, knew who he'd hit.

"Anything more, Marshal?" the magistrate asked. When the marshal shook his head, the magistrate said, "Then court's adjourned."

Hall and Hanaway halted at the gate to let a heavy-set man in townsman's clothes come through. He said, "Afternoon, Harry," and Hall replied, "How are you, Judge?"

Sheriff Canning was standing by the door, thumbs hooked in his belt. As the two men came abreast him, Canning said, "Better not leave yet, Harry. Your client's under arrest."

Hall pulled up so abruptly that Hanaway bumped into him. "On what charge?"

"Assault and battery—in Kittrick county, not in the town of Kittrick." He held out the warrant which Hall accepted.

"Who's the complainant?" Hall asked.

Hanaway said, "Why, Dave Reeves, Harry."

Canning said, "Come along," and headed for the gate in the railing.

Hanaway looked at the bench. The heavy-set man was sitting in the chair vacated by the magistrate. Hall said in a low tone of voice, "This can be a rough one. Anything I need to know?"

"You know it all."

Canning was waiting as the judge gaveled the courtroom to order. The sheriff led Hall and Hanaway to the bench where the judge, looking at Hall, said, "Your client understands this is not the magistrates' court he just appeared before, but a county court."

Hall nodded. "If it please the court, may I address the sheriff before this hearing begins?"

"Is it about something relevant to his hearing?"

"Very much so."

"Then go ahead."

Hall turned to Canning. "I ask that Dave Reeves be put under arrest. My client will sign the complaint."

Canning asked coldly, "What are your charging him with?"

"Attempted theft of a hundred shares of Consolidated stock. He's in the courtroom, so you won't have to hunt for him."

"I won't even try, unless you can produce a witness," Canning answered.

Hall turned to the judge. "Your Honor, I ask that the charges against my client be dropped. If the alleged assault and battery took place, it was only because Hanaway was trying to get back his stock certificates. And there are no witnesses to the alleged assault and battery."

The judge cleared his throat and said with apparent good humor, "Harry, you are arguing your case before the hearing has even opened. Your request for dimissal of the charges is denied because the prosecution has a witness that must be heard. Now, take your seats, please."

He gaveled the courtroom to order and read the charges. Dave Reeves was called to the witness stand. He was wearing his western costume, and he related how he had found Hanaway in the Consolidated office demanding as a Consolidated stockholder that he be shown the books. Reeves said he was shown the shares of stock and asked to keep them so their validity could be verified. This was when Hanaway assaulted him.

When he was finished, Hall rose and said, "Your Honor, when you borrow a man's stock certificates for verification you don't just put them in your pocket. You give him a receipt listing the number of shares and the issue number of the shares and the date received."

"He never gave me time to write out his receipt," Dave said. "I was on my way to do it when he jumped me."

Dave was dismissed and Walters from Consolidated was put on the stand. He told the exact truth. He'd heard a heavy thump coming from Dave's office, investigated, found Dave on the floor and Hanaway seated. Hanaway thought Dave had had an epileptic fit and Walters did too. He soon recovered, Walters said, and Hanaway asked to see the books, a right he was entitled to.

Hall rose and asked, "Did you see Hanaway hit Reeves?"

"I did not."

"Then he could have had an epileptic fit?"

"For all I know," Walters said. The Judge dismissed him.

Now the judge leaned forward, hands clasped before him and regarded Hanaway. "Since I saw you fined for a brawling earlier this afternoon, I'm wondering what sort of man you really are. One thing is certain. You are a troublemaker and you rely on violence to get your way. I believe you should be taught a lesson." He paused, so as to emphasize what was to follow. "By order of this Court, you are found guilty as charged and are directed to pay a fine of five hundred dollars to the clerk of Kittrick County. If you are unable to pay this fine, you will be locked up and will work out your fine at the rate of two dollars a day."

Hall had lunged halfway to his feet when Hanaway put an iron grip on his elbow. Hall sank back in his chair, and looked at Hanaway, unable to hide his fury.

"I've got it and I'll pay it," Hanaway said.

"It's illegal and a damned outrage!" Hall said.

"But the information I got brought Carrie and Neva over to our side. Let's forget the fine."

XIII

Dave Reeves headed straight for the bank from the courthouse. Although the bank was closed, his knock on the door brought the cashier, who let him in.

Ben heard the knock from his office and knew who it was. The news Dave would bring, and it would be good, had lost its interest for Ben in the light of the day's happenings. At the soft knock on the door, Ben called, "Come in, Dave."

Reeves stepped inside, a broad smile on his ferret's face. Taking off his hat, he moved toward the leather-covered arm chair, sank into it and said, "Well, we got him, Ben. A five-hundred-dollar fine."

"And he paid?"

Reeves nodded. "His lawyer was mad enough to choke."

"Hanaway too?"

"No. He didn't seem to mind it."

"So Walters testified?" At Reeves's nod, Ben said, "Good. Now I can fire him."

However, Ben wasn't wholly satisfied with the way this had gone. Earlier this afternoon he had talked with Bill Sylvester, the county judge. Ben had wanted Hanaway fined a thousand dollars, but Sylvester had argued against that amount. Hall, he said, would appeal it and win a reduction, thus discrediting Sylvester and inviting opposition in the next election. Sylvester was too good a man for Ben to lose, so he'd given in. Still, Ben wished he could have wiped out Hanaway's five hundred dollars and have him jailed for a while.

But this was only a minor irritation compared to what he would very likely face this evening. For he had come to his decision that he should get rid of

Dave immediately. As soon as one fact—the keystone of the arch—was slipped into place.

"Anna said she's expecting me for supper. I suppose we better get along," Ben said.

He collected the mass of papers on his desk in one pile, rose, then gestured to the pile and said sourly, "Hell, I'll have to spend half the morning at the county clerk's office getting these notarized."

Dave rose too. "Why don't you take them with you now and sign them after supper? I'll take them to the courthouse in the morning. They know your signature there."

Ben frowned and looked at the papers, then smiled and glanced at Dave. "I've got a better idea than that. What's the use of having a town and county named Kittrick after your old man if you can't ask a favor? I'll have the clerk bring his stamp here in the morning." He paused, as if musing, then went on, "Funny thing, Kittrick County was named after my dad. The county to the west of us was named after a river, Rio Blanco. The county to the east was named after a saint, San Isbel. They do crazy things like that back in Illinois? What's the name of the county Freeport's in?"

"Monroe County, named after President Monroe, they told us in school," Dave said without any hesitation.

That did it for Ben. Anna said Coxwell, Dave said Monroe, and the county's name was neither.

He picked up his hat from the rack, led the way through the lobby and unlocked the door. After relocking it from the outside, he turned and saw beyond Dave that his buggy was waiting.

"Your horse at the stable? Or do you want to drive out with me?" Ben asked.

"I'll pick him up and catch up with you."

Ben climbed into the buggy and put his horse in motion as Dave headed for the feed stable. He was glad to be alone, for he discovered that in the last few minutes he had become dangerously angry—dangerous because this evening would require a cool head. When was the best time to break the news? He wondered, and answered himself. After supper, of course.

He was aware that he risked losing Anna tonight, but he didn't think he would. If Anna and Dave were not brother and sister, there was no reason why they shouldn't go their separate ways, once their swindle was uncovered. And Ben had more to offer Anna than Dave. Ben hoped it was that simple.

Dave caught up with the buggy halfway to the ranch, and since conversation was difficult because of the racket of horse hooves and buggy tires on the rocky road, they traveled in silence. The day's heat still hung on, and the desert landscape shimmered in the distance.

They left the horses with José and walked under the cottonwoods toward the big gray house. Depending on what happened tonight, he might be selling the house soon, Ben thought.

Anna was waiting for them in the living room with drinks on a tray atop a table. She kissed Ben in front of Dave, then, because the house was shaded by the trees, she lighted the lamps against the dusk while Ben made the drinks.

The small talk of Hanaway's two hearings and fines vaguely irritated Ben. Never a modest man, Dave managed to make it sound as if he had pulled the whole thing off by himself.

After the second drink, Lupe called them to supper. It was a good one but Ben found he wasn't hungry. Anna, in her navy-blue long-sleeved dress that made her hair seem paler, had never looked more beautiful to him. He had never seen her angry and he wondered if he would tonight.

In the living room again, Lupe served them their coffee, then halted by the dining room doors and said good night. She closed the doors after her, leaving them to themselves. Ben went over to the drink tray, poured a dollop of whiskey in his coffee and sat down on the sofa beside Anna. He didn't know it but he'd been frowning.

Anna hugged his arm and said, "Something's bothering you, Ben. Is it that Hanaway business?"

"Not exactly," Ben answered. He looked at her now. "Anna, didn't you tell me this noon that Freeport, Illinois, was it Coxwell County?"

Anna looked at Dave, whose face was impassive because Ben was looking at him now.

"Why, yes, I did," Anna said.

Dave laughed suddenly. "Sis, you never were very bright with the schoolbooks. Coxwell County is the next county east. Don't you remember what was carved over the courthouse door? Monroe County Courthouse, silly sister."

Anna put her hands to her cheeks and said, "Oh, I do remember." She looked at Ben blushing. "Dad was selling farms all over. Everytime he had to go over to Bell Plaines to register a deed or something at the Coxwell County Courthouse, he'd take me along for the drive. I was mixed up."

"So Freeport is in Monroe County?"

Dave asked curiously, "Why does it matter, Ben?"

"Because both of you are lying," Ben said flatly. "Freeport is the county seat of Stephenson County."

Ben watched Dave's frown. "How would you know that?" Dave asked.

"Because that shyster Harry Hall got a telegram from the sheriff of Stephenson County. From Freeport."

Anna asked in a small voice, "Why would the sheriff send him a telegram, Ben?"

"In answer to the one Hall sent him. Would you like to know what the sheriff's telegram said?" At Anna's barely perceptible nod, Ben looked at Dave who shrugged indifferently. Ben went on implacably. "In the county tax records no Reeveses are recorded. No Reeveses in the birth records. And there are no Reeveses buried in any cemeteries in the county." He paused, watching the consternation in Anna's pale face. "If you're to be real swindlers, you'd better change your names to Smith. That'll be harder to trace."

68

Dave said sharply, "I'd like to see that telegram, Ben."

"Ask Hall or Hanaway for it. I know all I need to know from it. That you're liars. And that you aren't brother and sister."

"But we are brother and sister. We were born in ..."

"Enough!" Ben said roughly. "You'll only lie yourselves deeper into trouble." He addressed Dave now. "You're through at Consolidated. Don't go near the mine again. Don't come near me again. Move out of here tomorrow. And now," he added brutally, "as my mother used to say when I was bad, go to your room. I want to talk with Anna."

A white-faced Dave rose, skirted the sofa and went into the hall at the far end of the room.

Ben moved away from Anna on the sofa, put his back against the arm, crossed his heavy legs and faced her. She half faced him and, from the almost fearful expression on her face, Ben knew she was close to tears.

"Through lying?" he asked with gentleness.

Anna only nodded, watching him.

"You aren't brother and sister, are you?" Still gentle.

Anna began to cry, handkerchief to her eyes.

"Are you?" Ben pushed.

Anna said forlornly, "No."

"Now, stop your sniffling," Ben ordered. "I'm not going to scold you—not now or ever. I'm not going to prosecute you or Dave. I'm not even going to ask you why you did it." He fell silent as Anna tried to stifle her sobs. "Anna, look at me."

Wiping the tears from her eyes, she looked at him. Even in tears she was so heartbreakingly beautiful that Ben wanted to take her in his arms, but he knew she would break down again if he did.

"Did you hear what I just said?"

"I heard," she said, looking at him.

"Anna, I love you more than anything in the world. You've got to stay with me."

Anna's look was now one of disbelief. "You—you aren't sending me away with Dave?"

"No. I'll never send you away. I've promised you we will be married and we will."

She moved over to him and came into his arms, burying her face in his shoulder. "Oh, Ben, I love you. I don't deserve you for what I've done."

Ben stroked her hair as he said, "We love each other. We'll belong together until we die."

"Oh, yes, Ben. Yes."

When Ben had kissed her goodbye at the door, Anna closed the door and put her back to it. She was still half stunned by Ben's forgiveness and his declaration of love. A half hour ago the wreck of all her hopes was a reality, and then Ben had worked his miracle. Nothing was changed for her. The worst had happened and it turned out to be the best that could ever happen.

She walked out into the middle of the room and looked about as if she were seeing it for the first time. This was all hers, now, Ben had said. And then she caught sight of Dave standing in the doorway of the wing to which Ben had sent him.

Dave came slowly into the room and halted. They looked at each other in silence for a moment and then Dave said in a surly tone of voice, "My God, you look happy over what's happened."

"I am," Anna said. "Ben's keeping me on."

Dave stared at her in disbelief. "After what's happened? You can't mean that."

"But I do. Nothing has changed for me."

"Does he know about me?"

"He knows we aren't brother and sister. He can guess the rest."

"He won't have to. I'll write him," Dave said angrily.

"Oh, I think he knows. He just didn't ask," Anna said quietly. Then she smiled faintly. "Why are you mad, Dave? You knew I'd leave you for a man with money. I've always said I would. That's why I wouldn't marry you. You've known that from the beginning."

Dave came over to her and slapped her face so hard it half turned her head.

"Do that again and I'll tell Ben. He'll have you beat within an inch of your life."

"Do you love him like you say you love me?" Dave demanded.

"I love money. I love survival. I love being loved by a rich man. The rest doesn't matter."

"That doesn't answer my question," Dave said angrily.

"Then yes, I love him more than you. I just gave you the reasons," Anna said calmly. "You'd leave me in a second for any rich widow, and I wouldn't blame you. Then why are you blaming me?"

Her devastating candor held Dave speechless and she could see the anger draining from his face. It was over, she knew.

She moved past him saying, "Come, I'll help you pack."

XIV

For reasons Hanaway couldn't exactly define, he strapped on his gunbelt this morning. Maybe it was the way things had gone for him in two courts yesterday. Or maybe it was Ben Kittrick's rage upon reading the telegram from Freeport. Or maybe it was the parting words of Sheriff Canning to him as he and Hall had left the courtroom: "Next time you make trouble, Hanaway, it's jail for you, and I'll see the key gets lost." Too many people had too many reasons for disliking him and, since he was a stranger in a country that was proving hostile to him, he had better be prepared for further trouble.

Halfway through his breakfast of overdone eggs, tough steak and weak coffee, he had the feeling this was going to be a bad day. He felt restless and town-bound and, added to that, useless. He'd lost a nice chunk of money by belting two men who deserved it, but there was nothing to show for it. True, Carrie and Neva now knew that Ben was squandering their money, but nothing was changed.

When he'd finshed breakfast, he headed through the lobby and was almost at the door when he heard the clerk behind the desk call his name. Hanaway cut across to the desk and the clerk laid an envelope before him. "Mr. Kittrick's houseman left this for you."

Puzzled, Hanaway opened the envelope and took out a folded sheet of notepaper on which was written:

I have some news you might want to hear. Can you come by the house today at your convenience?

CARRIE KITTRICK

72

Again puzzled, Hanaway put the note in a pocket, thanked the clerk and headed for the veranda door. He had almost reached it when Dave Reeves entered the lobby, angling for the desk. They saw each other at the same time. Reeves stared past him and Hanaway, stride unbroken, ignored Reeves.

On the veranda Hanaway halted. Drawn up by the tie rail was a buckboard. From it a Mexican ranchhand was unloading a small trunk and a valise. Tied to the off-rear wheel of the buckboard was a saddled horse, Reeves's probably. The ranchhand shouldered the trunk, picked up the valise, climbed the veranda steps, passed Hanaway and entered the lobby. Hanaway turned and followed him to the lobby door. He saw Reeves put down a pen at the desk, receive a key and beckon to the ranchhand, then head for the stairs.

So Reeves was moving into the hotel, Hanaway thought, and he couldn't suppress a smile. Had Ben acted on the contents of the Freeport telegram? He was almost certain now what Carrie wanted to see him about—to give him the news.

Out on the street he headed for the feed stable, his day suddenly better. The fact that Reeves had registered at the hotel instead of waiting in the lobby for the northbound stage to make up meant he was staying in town. Certainly he'd made enough money off Ben to live there half a lifetime.

His dun saddled, Hanaway opened the corral gate and led his horse out. Mounted, he headed upstreet. The Mexican ranch hand now had the empty buckboard pulled up in front of the stable runway and the hostler was freeing the reins of Reeves's bay gelding from the tailgate. If Reeves were selling his horse, he'd do the dickering himself, Hanaway thought. Apparently, then, he was having the stable feed his horse, which confirmed that he was staying in town.

Hanaway headed for the bank corner and rode on to the Kittrick house in the already hot sun. Sarita answered his knock and told him Carrie was waiting for him on the patio. Rounding the corner of the porch, he could see Carrie sitting in the shade of the big cottonwood tree. She was dressed for riding in a divided skirt, man's double-breasted shirt and half boots, and was reading a book. She heard his boots on the flagstones, looked up, smiled and said, "Good morning, Hanaway," and put her book on the table beside her stetson. There was a kind of excitement in her voice and her eyes, Hanaway saw. He said good-morning and slacked into the chair next to hers.

Gesturing with his hat toward hers, he asked, "Been riding or are you going? I hope you're going and you want company."

"Going, and I do want company. But first I want to talk a lot."

"I'm listening." It would be cruel even to hint at what he thought she would talk about.

"Well, when Ben came down to breakfast this morning, Neva and I were trembling in our boots. We hadn't seen him since he left Hall's office and we didn't know what to expect."

"I reckon you wouldn't."

"Not an apology, certainly, because brother Ben never apologizes, but that's what we got. He said he was mad at our snooping and poking into his business, but when he thought it over he couldn't blame us. He hadn't realized how much money he'd paid Reeves. Then came the shocker."

Carrie shook her head as if still disbelieving, and went on. "The telegram from the sheriff convinced him they weren't brother and sister. He got them to admit it. So last night he fired Dave from the mine and gave him until today to get off the ranch."

"So it worked," Hanaway said quietly.

"Only thanks to you."

"What about Anna?"

"He's keeping her on at the ranch," Carrie said matter-of-factly but with a certain gentleness. "He's crazily in love with her, Hanaway. Did you know his marriage has been on the rocks for years?"

Hanaway nodded. "Hall hinted at it. All he had was town gossip."

Carrie frowned. "Ben's lonely. I don't think he cares that Anna lied to him or what she's been. And he just doesn't care what people think of him, and that includes his sisters."

"Maybe it won't include his sisters from now on. You sisters grew up some yesterday."

Carrie smiled uncertainly. "In a way, I suppose, but in exactly what way? I don't know."

"I think the shine is off Ben for Neva. Together, you two can make him account for your money he's spending and his reasons for it. You've got him on the run, so keep him moving."

Carrie shrugged. "If Neva keeps feeling the way she did this morning, I think we can. But where do we go from here?"

"Hall will be here. Let Neva ask him about her money problems. You should too."

"You mean you won't be here to help us?" Her voice was almost plaintive.

"No. My job's done, Carrie. If you girls give Harry Hall your powers of attorney, he can sit in on bank and mine meetings. He'll keep Ben in line. That's all you asked for in your letter to your Uncle Jeff, wasn't it?"

Carrie nodded assent, almost with reluctance. "When do you go?"

"In a couple of days, looks like."

Carrie sighed and rose. "Then we better make the best of the time you've got left. Sarita will make us sandwiches. Where do you want to ride?"

"Anywhere out of sight of town. I'm sick of it," Hanaway said, rising.

"To get really sick of it you have to live here," Carrie said with a false cheerfulness.

"Then leave it. You've got the money."

Carrie looked at him a silent moment. "Yes, I have. But there's a half-crazy woman upstairs. There's a bully of a brother living with a kept woman. There's a child sister. Who'll hold things together if I don't?"

Hanaway nodded gravely. "No argument."

As Carrie turned to head for the house, Hanaway

75

said, "When you're ready, Carrie, stop by for me at Hall's office. I want to tell him about Dave and Ben."

"Yes, he should know what his telegram did for us."

They parted and Carrie went around the back of the house, found Steve in the tack room by the corral, ordered her horse saddled, then went back to the kitchen. As she and Sarita made sandwiches for their lunch, Carrie thought of Hanaway's news that he'd be leaving in a couple of days. It was true that the job he promised Uncle Jeff he'd do was finished. He'd come in and quietly but stubbornly rearranged their lives and would soon go, leaving them in the hands of a competent Harry Hall. It didn't seem right that, after all he'd done for her and for Neva, he should just shake hands with them and disappear. Why, she knew nothing about him, even. Well, she'd remedy that on today's ride, she thought.

Saddlebag packed with sandwiches and canteen, she went through the house. Steve was waiting at the front steps with her black mare. He tied on the saddlebag, then gave her a hand up.

"Who's sidin' you, Miss Carrie?" Steve asked.

"Why, Mr. Hanaway, Steve."

Steve scowled. "Ben won't like that."

"Neither do you, but that's the way it is," Carrie said tartly.

She rode off under his disapproving gaze, heading for Harry Hall's office. Approaching it, she saw Hall and Hanaway in conversation at the tie rail in front of Hanaway's big dun.

As she reined in, Hall ducked under the tie rail and came over to her. "Morning, Carrie," he said, and smiled. "Hanaway's been telling me a fairy story. Is it true?"

Carrie looked from Hall to Hanaway. "Well, I've never caught him in a lie yet. Yes, it's true."

Hall grinned and shook his head. "My mother said there would be days like this, but only once in a while. Neva happy about it?"

"Just as happy as I am." She paused and then went on, "After Hanaway's gone, I think you'll be seeing a

76

lot of us, Harry. When I find out what Ben's paying Kelso, we're paying you the same amount to represent us. From now on, we fight Ben all the way."

"I'd do that for nothing," Hall said happily.

"But you will do it?"

"I don't have to think about it. Of course."

After they had parted with Hall and turned toward Main Street, Hanaway said, "Where we headed, Carrie?"

"Behind the mine there's a trail up the Flattops. It's nice up there and you can see almost to Mexico. You can see town from there too, but we don't have to look at it."

Along the dusty mine road they talked of Hall and what he could do for the Kittrick sisters. A mile outside of town they saw a buggy headed toward them. As it drew closer, they both recognized Mr. Walters, Consolidated's bookkeeper. There was a wooden crate on the seat beside him and Carrie held up her hand and reined in her mare.

Walters pulled up his buggy, took off his hat and said, "Morning, Miss Carrie. Hello, Hanaway. Headed for the mine?"

"Past it and up the Flattops, Mr. Walters." She looked at the crate beside him, and could see it held clothes, boots, ledgers, eyeshades, bottle of ink and miscellaneous office gear. She said then in a joking way, "You look like you're headed for a rummage sale, Mr. Walters. Where is it?"

"No, I'm just moving my personal belongings." His tone of voice was defensive but firm.

"Oh, where?"

"Out. Don't you know?" Carrie moved her head in negation and Walters went on, "I'm dismissed, as of this morning." He reached in the pocket of his jacket, pulled out a folded piece of paper and extended it to Carrie. "From Ben. I think he didn't want to face me."

Carrie made no move to take the note. She looked at Walters and asked, "Over Hanaway's visit?"

"No stated reason, but that would be my guess."

Carrie said gently, "Turn your buggy around, Mr. Walters. You are still working for Consolidated. My sister and I assure you."

Walters looked bewildered. He said, in a tentative sort of way, "But Ben is president of the company, Miss Carrie."

"Maybe he is. Still Neva and I can outvote him, and we just have, so turn your rig around, Mr. Walters."

"But I can't go back. Sid Herndon fired me."

"I'll talk to Sid. Now, you follow us." She put the mare in motion and Hanaway fell in beside her. She was so mad that her hand holding the reins was shaking. Looking at Hanaway, she said, "How am I doing? Ben will be furious, but Mr. Walters has been with us since I can remember."

"My hundred shares are behind you," Hanaway said drily. They both laughed and Carrie relaxed a little. She looked back and saw that Walters had turned his buggy and was following them and she wondered what she could say to Sid Herndon who was only following orders in firing Walters.

At the mine, Carrie gestured toward the office building and then, looking beyond it, she saw Herndon talking to a man standing in the open doorway of the hoist shacks. "There he is," Carrie said to Hanaway and pointed.

Herndon had seen Carrie and, breaking off the conversation, he headed across the hard-packed caliche toward them. He was a burly man wearing the same rough clothes, boots and wool hat as his poorest miners.

Halting between them, he said, "Morning, Carrie. Never see you any more." His scarred and craggy face broke into a smile. A man of perhaps fifty, he had a quiet character.

"Good morning, Sid." She gestured to Hanaway. Mr. Herndon, Mr. Hanaway."

"Seems like I've heard of you," Herndon said to Hanaway, then he moved over and they shook hands. He turned back to say something to Carrie when he saw Walter's buggy pull up at the tie rail in front of the office. Both Carrie and Hanaway looked over at the buggy and Carrie said, "I turned him around, Sid. This just can't happen."

"It shouldn't, but it was orders from the boss, Carrie."

"It *won't* happen. You don't use a man for fifteen years, then throw him away like a worn-out pair of slippers."

"Tell Ben. He's the man I work for."

"I intend to," Carrie said firmly. She thought a moment, then asked, "Is Walters a good man at his job, Sid?"

"There can't be a better one. If he's ever made a mistake with our books, it sure got by me."

Carrie came to her decision then. She asked, "You know who owns Consolidated stock, don't you?"

"The Kittricks, split three ways." He looked at Hanaway and smiled. "Except for a piddling one hundred shares owned by the man on your left."

Carrie said immediately, "All right. Neva and Hanaway are with me. We want Walters to stay. We want him to keep the books in our interest, the majority interest."

Herndon shrugged. "Hell, Carrie. I only work for you Kittricks. Ben's president of the corporation. If you want to unvote him or disvote him or vote in a new president, that's up to you."

"Then give Mr. Walters back his old job. We've voted."

"Then tell Ben I fired him and you two girls rehired him." He smiled then. "I hope you win that one, Carrie, I really do."

"We'll win it, Sid. Now, do you tell Mr. Walters he's still working for us, or do I?"

"I do. I don't want to get fired for refusing."

They both laughed, Herndon gave them a careless wave and headed for Walters, who was still sitting in his buggy waiting for the decision.

Carrie looked at Hanaway and for the second time today she asked, "How am I doing?"

79

Hanaway smiled faintly and said, "You don't have to ask."

Carrie led the way past the hoist shack and picked up the road and their climb up the Flattops. The road was one long gradual slant up the mountainside, a dugway the mine cut out to get logs for timbering from up in the higher reaches of the San Isbel. Carrie was silent for a long time and Hanaway, grateful to be outdoors and astride a horse once more, was content.

When they stopped to blow their horses, Carrie said, "Tell me more about you and Uncle Jeff. I know you were neighbors, but how did that happen?"

"Happen is the word for it," Hanaway said after a pause. "I was an orphan, kind of." He went on to say he couldn't remember much about his parents who both died between his seventh and eighth birthdays. He was taken in by his father's brother, a lawyer. When he got all the schooling available, he began to read law in his uncle's office and to attend court, but soon decided this was not for him. He was meant to live out of doors and work with his hands.

With his uncle's approval he struck out on his own. Leaving the plains, he instinctively headed for mountain country. He'd hunted wild horses for a spell. A complete drifter, he'd worked for both big and small spreads. Always the youngest of any crew, he had always been worked the hardest.

He'd hit Jeff Kittrick's spread at roundup time. In a country short of men he was hired immediately. After they'd driven the beef to the railroad, Jeff Kittrick, instead of paying him off, asked if he wanted to work for him. Hanaway agreed, asking to be paid off in beef. He was tired of taking care of other men's cattle. After five years with Jeff, the last three as foreman of a five-man crew, he bought land from Jeff and, with his small herd, struck out on his own. He was through being a saddle tramp. Under his own roof for the first time in his life, he'd "made out all right."

They were climbing again as Hanaway finished. Carrie had listened in silence with only an occasional nod. Now she said, "There's a word for you. You're a 'loner,' aren't you?"

"I reckon that says it," Hanaway agreed, and regarded her soberly. "You're pretty much of a 'loner' yourself."

"With Ben and Neva against me, I've had to be. But maybe that's changed now."

When they reached the crest of the road, Hanaway was surprised to see the flattops were sparsely timbered with cedar and piñon trees stretching west until San Isbels shouldered up and displaced them with ponderosa.

They headed north, spooking half a dozen bunches of quail that skittered out of the way, refusing to take wing for only a pair of horses. On the rim which overlooked the arroyo-scarred desert below, they found an old piñon tree that offered shade. His back against the trunk, Hanaway watched Carrie spread the cloth and lay out their lunch. She moved with quick grace, absorbed in what she was doing but frowning as if in thought.

"Wondering what Ben will say about Walters, Carrie?" Hanaway asked.

Carrie looked up, startled, and then she nodded. "You are a great mindreader. Yes, I am." She paused and, still looking at him, said, "I wonder if I'd have had the courage to turn him around if you hadn't been with me."

"Yes. By instinct. You didn't want to see a good man wronged. I had nothing to do with it."

"But I've watched good men wronged before." She hesitated, then said quietly, "I think you've taught me to fight back."

"Ben's a bully, and any bully will take water if he's stood up to."

They ate their lunch then and afterward Carrie talked quietly. From under their tree they could see in three directions and Carrie described the country. To the east, so distant a blue haze almost obscured it, was a long jumble of mountains, the Vultures. Far south lay the Malpais, the badlands, a waste of black volcanic lava debris, while to the west and infinity beyond where the horses were grazing lay the Sacramento.

"Everything else is mesquite and every kind of cactus I can't name," Carrie finished.

Hanaway was looking at his big dun some yards away. The dun's head was up, ears almost pointed forward.

"We'll be having company," Hanaway said.

Carrie looked at him in puzzlement. "Where?"

"That's what our horses are telling us."

Hanaway rose, brushed the piñon needles from his seat and looked off to the north. Presently a horse and rider appeared from behind a tree, head bent searching for tracks, and Hanaway looked down at Carrie. "It's Ben," he said, and saw the surprise and something close to fear come into her face.

When Ben approached, Hanaway could see that his horse was lathered. As he came closer, and reined up a few yards from them, Hanaway saw that his face was flushed, his mustache dripping perspiration. His shirt clung to his body in the midday heat.

He came striding over to them, lifting his hat and wiping his forehead with his shirtsleeves.

"Bring any water, Carrie?"

Carrie, still seated, handed him the canteen which he drank from immediately. He did not so much as look at Hanaway.

"You seem in pretty much of a hurry. Has anything happened?" Carrie asked.

Ben capped the canteen and glared at her. "Has anything happened? God, what gall you have to ask that!"

"Is this about Walters? Because if it is, you've come a long way for nothing. I won't change my mind, Ben," Carrie said flatly.

"I've changed your mind for you," Ben said angrily. "I rode out to the mine to see if Sid had obeyed my orders. He told me what happened. I went into the office and fired Walters personally. He's gone for good."

Carrie's blue eyes flashed with anger. "I wouldn't be too sure of that."

"You better be. As long as I'm president of the board, Walters is out."

Carrie was silent for long seconds, studying her brother, and then she asked, almost sweetly, "Dearest brother, how would you like to face a stockholders' suit for recovery of the money you paid Dave Reeves? Also for fraud, since you covered it by charging it to geological exploration. And how would you like it if Neva and I voted to throw you out as president of the bank and the mine?" After a pause she added, ever so gently, "I think you're going to rehire Walters with a comfortable raise. And I think you'll keep him hired."

To Hanaway, Ben's face was a study in surprise, anger and total frustration. For the first time since he'd ridden up he looked at Hanaway, the point of whose shoulder leaned against the tree trunk.

"This your idea?" Ben asked roughly.

"Ask your sisters."

Ben's hot glance shifted to Carrie. "Was it?"

"He only pointed out you're outvoted, Ben. You always were after we came of age, only we paid no attention. We are now. You pay for your little dolly with your own money, not ours. Harry Hall will attend all bank and mine meetings. He'll review all bank loans and property sales. He'll do all this because we're retaining him as our lawyer. You've got your Jim Kelso, we've got our Hall—with proxies for more than two thirds of the mine stock and just under two thirds of the bank stock."

By the time Carrie had finished, there was a blazing rage in Ben's dark eyes. When he could speak it was with a savage sarcasm. "So the Kittrick money will be handled by two silly girls and a shyster. Do you think you could find a clerk's job for me?"

Carrie laughed then. "No, neither Neva nor I want to learn to smoke cigars and drink straight whiskey and sit behind a desk. You'll be running things like you always did—only from now on you're being watched, big brother. We need you, but we need Harry Hall too."

"But I make the decisions," Ben said flatly.

"All yours and welcome to them, once Harry Hall approves."

Hanaway could see that Ben hated all of this but that there was nothing he could do about it. Carrie had allowed him to save face, but on the sisters' terms. Are you listening, Uncle Jeff? Hanaway thought. Ben was speaking to him again, a sneer in his voice.

"Well, Hanaway, which of my sisters is going to marry you?"

Hanaway looked down at Carrie. Her lips parted in surprise at the question, she shifted her glance from Ben to Hanaway.

His face contained, Hanaway was silent a few seconds, thinking how Ben's question was put. Then he said soberly, "Which sister is going to marry me? I don't know yet, Ben. Up to now neither one has asked me for my hand. They're both nice girls, but I'll have to say no to one of them, won't I?"

Laughter exploded from Carrie. When she could talk, she choked out, still laughing, "You're so beautiful, Hal. Will you marry me?"

Laughing too, Hanaway looked down and scuffed the ground with his boot in mock shyness. "This is too quick, Carrie. Will you give me time to think it over?"

Ben roared angrily, "Goddamnit, stop that!"

This brought a fresh howl of laughter from Carrie. His own shoulders shaking in silent laughter, Hanaway looked at Ben. His sweaty face was livid with anger.

"Hanaway, you're through here. Get out of town or I'll run you out!" He turned, went back to his horse, mounted, spurred his horse viciously and rode off at a gallop.

Carrie bent her head, put her arms around her midriff and said, "My stomach hurts from laughing." She dabbed with her handkerchief at her eyes, blotting away the tears of laughter. She raised her head, arched her back briefly and, smiling now, she looked at Hanaway. "Ben hates to be laughed at. He'll never forgive me, but I couldn't help it."

Hanaway sat down now and put his back against the tree trunk, his smile lingering. "By now I reckon Ben's a little sorry he came up here." He looked fondly at Carrie. "Everything's laid on the line now, Carrie. That was one hell of a job you did on him."

"Well, it's out of the way." She looked at him with an expression of curiosity. "I couldn't have done it alone, and that's the second time I've said that today. Thanks for just being here."

Hanaway dipped his head in acknowledgment, then said, "Time's a wastin', girl. Let's look at some more country."

XV

The poker game in the hotel's bar was ended, with Dave Reeves the winner as usual. He'd bought the losers a drink and they'd gone, leaving only Dave and the bartender in the room that was slowly clearing of tobacco smoke. The bartender was at the table the players had just left, putting the chips and cards in their cases and yawning while he did so.

Dave heard rather than saw a man come up to the bar beside him. Looking up from his drink, he saw the sheriff standing there.

"Hello, Wes. You keeping the cork on the town tonight?"

"Yeah," Canning said. "That jackleg lawyer says I can't, but nobody knows it but him."

The bartender came behind the bar, stowed the poker gear under it, then came up to them. There was a half-filled bottle in front of Reeves; he lifted it and asked, "Suit you?" and when Canning nodded, Reeves said to the bartender, "Another glass. We'll sit at the table."

Canning picked up the glass and pitcher of water and he and Reeves, bottle in one hand, drink in the other, moved over to the table just vacated and sat down.

The sheriff thumbed his hat to the back of his head as Reeves poured a generous drink in both their glasses.

"Ben says you've quit Consolidated," Canning said.

Dave knew Ben wouldn't say he'd fired him, for then he would have to admit he'd been taken. He said easily, "Well, a year ago Sis and me were headed for California to visit our brother. I hope he hasn't been waiting all this time at the stage station." He joined in

Canning's laughter. "No, I'm just getting restless. Want to see some new country."

Canning nodded absently, but his pale eyes held a faint worry. "Just what the hell is eating old Ben? He came ramming into the office just before I locked up for supper. Said he wanted this Hanaway run out of town no matter how." He frowned. "Hell, we've got him fined twice, but we can't chase him out of town unless he makes real trouble. He even told Hanaway he'd run him out."

Reeves came alert. "What did Hanaway say to that?"

"Ben didn't say. He likely said, 'Just try and do it.'"

They talked about ways to trap Hanaway into causing trouble, but Reeves wasn't really paying attention; his mind was on what Canning had just told him and he wanted to think about it. When Canning rose, still undecided about baiting Hanaway, he thanked Dave for the drink and went out.

Dave paid for the drinks, then crossed the lobby, heading for the stairs. In his room he shucked out of his coat, lit up a cigar, swung the rocking chair so it faced the bed, slacked into it and propped his feet up on the bed.

So Ben had told Hanaway to get out of town; moreover, Ben had told Canning about it. Therein lay the ready-made motive to bring about Ben's death and lay the blame on Hanaway.

For Reeves, after a sleepless night and a day of angry brooding, had decided to kill Ben. Last night's brutal humiliation at Ben's hands was something he could never forgive nor even forget. In one unbelievable hour Ben had contemptuously stripped him of his job, his pride and his greedy woman whom he loved in spite of everything. Even the thought brought a sick anger to him.

He was suddenly aware of a sharp pain in his right hand. He looked down at it and saw that, in his angry reverie, he had balled up his lighted cigar in his clenched fist.

Dropping the cigar, he rose, swearing, and ground

it into the floor. He licked the burn which was hurting, then took out his handkerchief, wrapped it around his palm and sat down, again putting his feet on the bed.

The pain of the burn had, in a way, brought him back to his senses. He tried now to anticipate the consequences of Ben's death. First, Hanaway, the root cause of all his rotten luck, would be blamed for the bushwhack, caught, jailed and tried. Second, Anna would be thrown off the place after the funeral and she would return to him, since she would have nowhere else to go. They had plenty of money to live on, but not in this godforsaken hole.

There were several chancy angles involved, of course. Did the Kittrick sisters know he'd been fired? Probably. Then the thing for him to do was leave town openly and return secretly, not an easy job but possible and necessary. If he'd been seen to leave town, the shooting couldn't be blamed on him even by the Kittrick sisters.

Lastly, he must leave something at the scene of the shooting that would clearly connect Hanaway with the act. Well, he could do that too if he gave it some thought. But not tonight. It was late and he was tired and half drunk. He blew out the lamp and went to bed.

Next morning he got down to the dining room just before the doors were closed. The Mexican maids were already at work cleaning the rooms and he figured they'd be finished by the time he finished eating. Done with breakfast, he went over to the lobby desk, paid his bill, and asked that his luggage be brought down to be put on the northbound stage for Junction City.

"Will you see the driver?" he asked the clerk.

"Yes, Mr. Reeves. He always comes in for a drink before he heads out."

Reeves put a half eagle on the desk. "Give this to him and tell him to dump my gear at the Junction City Hotel, will you?"

"You're not going on the stage?"

"No. I've got a horse I won't give up. I'll ride him to Junction City and then I'm heading north. For good."

"Well good luck, sir. I'll see the driver gets this."

Again in his room, Reeves waited until the Mexican handyman came for his luggage. Afterward he picked up his shellbelt from the bed and strapped on his gun, then went out into the corridor and halted, looking in both directions. At the far end of the corridor to his right, the Mexican maid, broom in hand, was locking the door to a room. She did not see him, since she turned the other way, opened a door, and took the backstairs to the kitchen.

Reeves walked down the corridor to room ten, no answer and then tried the door. It was locked. He reached in his pocket for his key ring, drew it out and looked at it, realizing for the first time that he had not left his office and house key with Anna. It was too late for that now, and it didn't matter anyway. From the few keys on the ring, he separated a long shiny steel key whose half-inch point was bent at a right angle to its shaft: In half a lifetime spent in crime, both overt and covert, some of it in jails, he had acquired a knowledge of lock picking.

He inserted the bit of this improvised skeleton key in the keyhole and probed gently until he found the movable part of the lock, turned the bit, and heard the lock click. He opened the door then, went in, pocketed the key ring and closed the door.

A quick look told him the room had been made up. In the lone armchair by the window was a folded blanket; he moved over to it and lifted the upper half. Here, except for the clothes hanging on hooks on the wall in the far corner, was everything Hanaway had brought with him—razor, soap, washcloth, socks, neckerchiefs, comb and papers and a letter. What was there in this ordinary collection of possessions that would identify Hanaway? Papers, of course. He picked up a paper which turned out to be the Consolidated stock certificates he'd already seen; Hanaway wouldn't be carrying those. He picked up the next piece of paper and recognized it immediately. It was

Walter's report on what Reeves had been paid in thirteen months, written on stationery with the Consolidated imprint. Hanaway wouldn't be carrying that either. Next he found a paper that was already creased and rumpled, as if it had served its purpose and had been jammed into a hip pocket and been ridden on and sat on. He unfolded it and found it was a printed receipt form bearing an illegible signature and made out to Hanaway.

Reeves tossed it with the other papers and then something clicked. He retrieved it and examined it carefully and then he smiled. This was the receipt given by the county clerk to Hanaway for payment of his five-hundred-dollar fine. It was something a man would ram in his pocket and forget until he emptied his pockets. It was also something a man could lose and wouldn't miss, since it had no value.

Reeves pocketed the receipt, arranged the blanket as he had found it; let himself out into the empty corridor, locked the door, then headed for his room.

The stage had gone when he came down to the lobby carrying his blanket roll. He left it in a corner of the lobby, went out to the street and headed for the bank. There he drew out his balance—over five hundred dollars—shook hands with the clerk and said he was leaving for California. Afterward he went down to Brady's, bought a drink, then shook hands with the bartender and told him he was leaving. Back at the hotel, he picked up his blanket roll and shook hands with the clerk, then went into the bar and said goodbye to the bartender. At the feed stable he asked that his horse be saddled and then stepped into the office to say goodbye to the owner. All these farewells were to establish the fact that he'd left town around midday.

He rode north out of town but turned off on the road to Consolidated. He watched for a place where a rider or vehicle had left the road on its north side, and when he came to a set of buggy tracks leading off the road, he followed them. When they seemed to turn back toward the road, he left them and cut north. He had, he hoped, left the road unobtrusively. Of course he could have taken the stage road, but then he would have risked being sighted from the house by Lupe or Anna or José.

When he figured he was well past the house and to the west of it, he found a steep-walled arroyo. The sun heeled over enough so that the wall cast some shade, and Reeves dismounted in it, tied his horse to a protruding mesquite root, spread out his blanket in the shade and went to sleep.

He awakened at dark, rolled up his blanket and tied it behind the cantle, mounted and headed for the road. He remembered Ben's nightly routine when he reached the ranch. There were drinks, supper, some talk or reading in the living room, then Anna, who liked late hours, would go to her bedroom. Ben would go into the kitchen where Lupe always left a bottle and glasses on the counter, would mix himself a nightcap, then come back to the living room to sit in the most comfortable chair and drink it before he joined Anna in her bedroom. He won't join you tonight, Sis, he thought, and then he wondered what Anna would do tonight after it happened.

The shot, he knew, would bring José. If it didn't, Anna's screams would. José would put Ben's body in a bedroom, then ride in to report the murder to Sheriff Canning who would come out to investigate. Hopefully, he would find the clues awaiting him. Lupe would sit up all night with a shattered Anna. Canning would be back at the ranch at daylight. If he'd missed the soiled handkerchief with the county clerk's receipt wadded up in it, he would find it then.

A quarter of a mile from the house he dismounted and tied his horse to a fence post of the horse pasture. It was a moonless night but he could see from one fence post to the next and he walked along the fence line, headed for the lamplit house.

The lamp in the kitchen was turned low, which meant Lupe was finished for the day and had gone to her quarters. The lamp in the living room was still burning, however. Skirting the kitchen, he wound up in the blackness of the big cottonwoods. Moving slowly and carefully, he went from one trunk to the next until he had reached a spot where he could look through the big many-paned window into the living room. Anna was seated on the sofa reading a book. Ben was sitting in the big chair by the lamp reading a newspaper.

Reeves leaned against a tree and waited. He knew he couldn't be seen from the house even if they both came to the window. After a minute or so Anna yawned, put her open book face down on the sofa and spoke to Ben. He lowered his paper, said something and then Anna rose and left for the bedroom.

Reeves moved toward the window, pulling on his gloves now. Two panes in the left lower corner of the window had been removed to make room for a cooler. Clean burlap had been tacked in the space where the panes had been, and its bottom edge rested in a tin tank holding water. Catclaw, with their vicious barbs, had been planted in front of the cooler to keep birds and vermin from fouling the water.

Reeves took out a pocketknife, opened the blade and waited, watching Ben. He hated that face with its sullen arrogance and he supposed it would look the same even in death. He'd never know, because he'd be long gone when the funeral was held.

Ben threw the newspaper aside, rose and moved toward the kitchen. Reeves gave him only a second, then moved toward the cooler, knife in hand. The catclaw found him as he reached out with the knife, but he rammed his arm through, taking the pain, and slashed a diagonal hole in the cloth. When it fell away, he could see into the room. Pulling his arm free, he drew his gun and cocked its single action. Then, shifting it to his left hand, he drew from his jacket pocket the soiled red bandanna with the county clerk's receipt mashed inside it. Impaling the bandanna on the catclaw at waist level as if the thorns had plucked it out of his pocket, he shifted his gun to his right hand just before Ben came back into the room with a drink in hand.

He waited until Ben seated himself in the same chair, then he eased his right arm and gun through the catclaw, poking the gun through the burlap. It had to be this way and not through a windowpane which could deflect the bullet. The angle Ben's chair was facing wasn't good, but it would have to do. Reeves drew a deep breath, sighted on Ben's upper arm and part of his chest, and slowly squeezed the trigger.

The blast of the gun was deafening. Ben was wiped sideways out of his chair, carrying it with him.

Hurriedly now, Reeves yanked his arm away from the clinging barbs and walked swiftly into the stand of cottonwoods. He was past the kitchen when he heard Anna's screams. Wild shriek followed shriek.

Reeves was almost at the road when he heard the pounding of José. Halting, Reeves looked back. José, lighted lantern in hand, was running for the kitchen door, Lupe behind him. When they disappeared into the kitchen, Reeves holstered his gun, pocketed his gloves and made his quiet way toward his horse.

XVI

"Where were you last night, Hanaway?" Sheriff Canning asked wearily. He, Hanaway and Hall occupied all the chairs in the sheriff's small office. Canning sat in the desk swivel chair, back to his desk, while Hanaway and Hall sat in straight-backed chairs he had placed before him as if to welcome errant schoolboys.

"You could have asked me that in the dining room and let me finish my breakfast," Hanaway said mildly. "I was with Harry here until a little after nine. Then I went back to the hotel and went to bed."

"Did you stay there?"

"Unless I sleepwalked. Why?"

Canning's redshot amber eyes held a loathing he didn't try to hide. He said, "Funny you should ask me if we could pick up Hall on our way here. Were you expecting trouble?"

"You've never given me anything but trouble, Sheriff. Why shouldn't I expect it?" Hanaway said quietly.

Hall said impatiently, "Ask your questions, Wes. I haven't eaten."

"Neither have I," Canning growled, still looking at Hanaway, and now talking to him. "I don't believe you've heard that Ben Kittrick was gunned down at the Diamond K last night?"

"No, but I'm not surprised," Hanaway said.

"That's a hell of a thing to say!" Canning said angrily.

"It's a hell of a thing to *have* to say," Hanaway replied. "Is he dead?"

"You didn't stay to make sure?" Canning asked with quiet savagery.

"Well, well. May I have this dance?" Harry Hall cut

in. "Is Ben dead? And no, he didn't stay to make sure. I only want to know, too."

"He's likely dying," Canning said coldly. "His right shoulder's in little pieces. He lost a lot of blood. Doc says he may have the slug still in him. We couldn't find it on the floor or walls in the living room. Doc's almost sure he'll have to cut off the arm."

"Do the girls know?" Hanaway asked.

"I told them before I come for you."

"Why'd you come for me?"

"Did Ben threaten to run you out of town?" Canning countered. At Hanaway's nod, the sheriff went on, "You was trying to make sure he wouldn't do it when you drygulched him, wasn't you?"

Hall said scornfully, "That's not even worth an answer, Hanaway."

"Maybe this is," the sheriff said. He turned and picked up from the desk what his body had been hiding. It was a soiled red bandanna handkerchief. He held it out to Hanaway. "This yours?"

Hanaway took it, looked at it and handed it back. "Could be. I've got some like it."

Canning now extended the rumpled receipt from the county clerk. "Recognize this?"

Hanaway took the piece of paper, straightened it out, read it, frowned and said, "Yes, that's the receipt for the fine I paid the other day."

Hall reached out, took the receipt, read it, then looked at Canning. "Where'd you get this?"

"It was in the bandanna. The bandanna was snagged in the catclaw in front of the window Hanaway shot him through." To Hanaway he said jeeringly, "Now, try telling me how it got there."

"I can't," Hanaway said promptly.

"Just a minute," Hall cut in. He looked at Hanaway. "What'd you do with the receipt when you got it?"

"You were there. What did I do with it? Stuck it in my pocket, I reckon. It just didn't seem important, Harry."

Hall persisted. "When you clean out your pockets at

night, what do you do with the stuff you were carrying?"

"Toss it on my blanket roll."

"Then somebody must have broken into your room and taken it," Hall said.

Canning said sardonically, "Keep working at it, Harry. Ask him when he noticed it was missing. I'll bet you he can remember."

"No. I don't remember missing it," Hanaway said. "I don't know how it got where you found it. I've never been to Ben's ranch either. And I've never shot at a man unless he was about to shoot at me."

The sheriff rose and held out his hand to Hall who gave him the receipt. He put it in his shirt pocket, buttoned the flap, then said to Hanaway, "Take off your shellbelt."

"Are you arresting him?" Hall asked sharply. "If you are, what's the charge?"

Canning gave him a wolfish grin. "No, you don't, sonny. I'm holding him in jail until the district attorney makes the charge."

"Jim Kelso," Hal said with distaste. "He should disqualify himself because Ben is his client."

"That's for you lawyers and Judge Benson to figure out," Canning said, and held out his hand. "The shellbelt, Hanaway." When it was given to him, he put it on his desk, then said, "Follow me."

Hall said, "Lock me in with him. We have to talk."

Canning said, "You want to stay in there most of the day?"

"Why do I have to?" Hall asked.

In a voice rasping with exasperation, Canning said, "Because I damn well won't be here and you know it. I've got to round up Kelso and Judge Benson, and testify at the preliminary hearing. Why don't you talk through the bars, then you can leave when you're done."

"Better than good," Hall said cheerfully. "We won't have you around, acting like a short-fuse sheriff."

Canning gave him a baleful look, took keys and handcuffs from the desk drawer, went out into the corridor, waited for the two men to follow him, then locked the door of his office. The basement stairs let on to a six-cell jailblock. All the barred cell doors were swung open. Canning chose the cell at the foot of the stairs and Hanaway went inside. The sheriff hand-cuffed him to one of the bars dividing the cells, close enough to the metal cot so that he could sit down. Afterward he went out, locked the barred door and, without a word of parting, went up the stairs.

Hanaway was the only prisoner. He looked about him. The metal cot with its shuck mattress and navy-blue blanket that he was sitting on, and the bucket and dippers beside it, were the cell's only furnishings. The cell was clean and he hoped bugless. It was cool enough now for his duck jacket to be comfortable. Turning his head, he heard and saw Hall pacing the narrow corridor in front of the cells, hands rammed in his hip pockets, head down in thought.

When Harry was even with him, Hanaway asked, "What'll the charge be, Harry?"

Hall didn't look up. "If Ben dies, murder. If he lives, attempted murder with a hell of a high bail that you can't meet. Kelso and Canning are Ben's chore-boys. They'll be out to get you. Benson's a good district judge, but then Ben was what you might call our First Citizen. He won't be easy on you."

Hall came up to the cell door and grasped a bar with each hand. "You thinking what I'm thinking?"

Hanaway slowly shook his head. "I'm not thinking yet, Harry. This happened too fast."

"All right. Who had the best reason for hating Ben?"

"Easy. Dave Reeves had a couple of good reasons. Ben booted him and busted up his partnership with Anna."

Hall nodded. "Think I'll snoop around some. See you later."

When Hall left, Hanaway leaned back against the dividing bar and swung a leg up on the blanket. The handcuff on his left wrist was tolerable. There was an irony in his predicament that didn't escape him. He

97

had planned on heading home today and for the best of reasons. Yesterday spent with Carrie had convinced him he was falling in love with her. He had seen her change from a rather uncertain and basically timid girl into a real woman. The way she had confronted Ben in Hall's office, the decision and her victory over him bespoke a generous girl with courage and character. She would make some man a good and loving wife, but not himself.

Last night after leaving Hall, he had paced his room, weighing decisions that lay ahead. If he asked her to marry him and she accepted—for he thought she was as fond of him as he was of her—there was the very real problem of where they would live. She'd been brought up in luxury and had money of her own. How could he take her north to his modest and isolated spread? She was a town girl. She would offer to add on buildings, land and breeding stock to the spread and he wouldn't accept her money because he wanted to work for these changes, not accept them as a gift from a rich wife.

There was the reverse side of the coin. What if they agreed to live in Kittrick, even agreed to live at Diamond K? They would have to buy up the leases and restock the range, all on Carrie's money. Eventually he would be a townsman, representing Carrie's interests along with Hall in the mine and bank, handling property, managing money he hadn't earned and didn't want. No. Even with love and kindness to each other they were a different breed. Better back off before the choice had to be made and there was still time.

And now this. If Ben died, he was in this cell until his trial, and that could be weeks and months away. He refused to think of that because nothing, not even around the-clock guard, could keep him here that long. He stretched out as best he could and slept.

He was wakened close to noon by the sound of Hall's footsteps on the stone stairs, and he sat up. Hall had something wrapped in newspaper in his hand. He came through the open door of the cell closet to

Hanaway's cot, thrust the package through the bars and said, "That's our dinner."

Hanaway took it, put it on the cot and asked, "Find out anything?"

"Yeah. None of it good." He told about checking the hotel first on the movements of Dave Reeves and learning that yesterday he had sent his luggage to Junction City on the late morning stage, leaving money to pay the driver to drop his gear at the Junction City Hotel. The driver confirmed this. Reeves would follow later because he owned a horse he didn't want to part with. The feed stable confirmed that he took out his horse before noon. The bank clerk said he had closed out his account before dinner.

"So he got out of town more than half a day before Ben was gunned down," Hall concluded gloomily.

"But on a horse," Hanaway said. "He could turn a horse around, couldn't he?"

"And come back and shoot Ben late at night." Hall scowled in thought.

"He'd be fairly sure I'd be in bed so nobody could give me an alibi, wouldn't he?"

Hall circled the cell in a kind of restless prowl, then looked at Hanaway and said, "He'd be taking a hell of a chance if anything went wrong."

"You said he's a gambler. And what chance is he taking?"

"If he's ever suspected, and he won't be, he's left a trail a child could follow. Sends his gear to the Junction City Hotel, says goodbye to three-four people, and rides out." He shook his head. "I don't think he did it, and I want to."

"He left that trail on purpose," Hanaway said with quiet conviction.

Hall stopped his pacing and came over to Hanaway. "You sound pretty sure. Why would he?"

Hanaway nodded, looked at Hall for a moment, then said, "Reeves didn't head for Junction City when he left here. He'll never see it again. He killed Ben and hit out on the long ride."

"But his gear—" Hall paused, his comprehension swift.

Hanaway continued, "With the money Ben paid him salted away, what does he care about a trunkful of clothes?"

Hall was by now nodding his agreement.

"That trunk and all those goodbyes were just to pull suspicion off him. There," Hanaway finished, "Give Judge Benson an earful at the hearing."

"No, I can't, for the simple reason the accused's lawyer is not allowed at a preliminary hearing. That's when the prosecution presents its reasons to the judge for arrest and detention. You'll be charged with attempted murder. You plead not guilty and demand, as your right, to be freed on bond."

"Can I bring up this business of Reeves at the hearing?"

"You could but it won't do any good. The judge may tell Kelso and Canning to investigate that possibility and they'll say they will but they won't. Then the judge will set a bond so high that you can't possibly meet it, so you're back in jail."

"Any more about Ben?"

"Only that he was brought in to Doc Price's today. I heard the arm goes. Now let's eat."

XVII

By the afternoon, both Carrie and Neva were lying down in their rooms. It had been a shattering day for them both, but especially so for Carrie. After Sheriff Canning's early morning visit, they had Steve drive them out to the ranch. Lupe let them in and led them back to the bedroom where Ben, still in his bloody clothes, lay stretched out on the bed, with Dr. Price sitting in a chair by his side. Ben was either sleeping or unconscious; he looked drained and ghastly pale. His shoulder was bandaged and Dr. Price put a finger to his lips for silence, rose, lifted the bandage to look for signs of new bleeding, then beckoned to them to follow him and led the way back to the living room.

Dr. Price was a tall, stooped man with an unruly shock of gray hair above a sad, hound's face made somewhat ridiculous by iron-rimmed half glasses that rode midway down his crooked nose. He was in shirtsleeves, cuffs rolled up, and he raised big hands to grasp his suspenders as he turned to them.

"I know. You want to know if he's alive. The answer is barely. We're in trouble."

Neva was silently crying. Carrie was dry-eyed, but beyond sorrow she felt a stifling anger.

Dr. Price went on. "I've decided on something risky, but I hope you'll agree. Ben shouldn't be moved but he's got to be. I've sent in a note to Brigham to bring out his hearse. It's the softest-riding wagon in town. We'll carry him out on his mattress."

"Where are you taking him, Dr. Price?" Carrie asked.

"The hospital room in my house. That's for two reasons. One is that he'll need constant attention, either from me or Mrs. Price." He hesitated, then plunged on. "The second is that I have to take off that arm."

The girls looked at each other in horror. Carrie's glance shifted to Dr. Price. "Do you—? I mean, is it absolutely necessary?"

"It's that or gangrene, Carrie." He put a hand on her shoulder. "I was a contract surgeon in the war, and I've done it many a time."

Carrie said bitterly, "If they catch the man that did it, I hope he hangs."

"Do you know who did it?" Neva asked.

"Oh, the sheriff claims he can prove it. "It's the same fellow that broke Ben's nose. I forget his name. Now, you two girls . . ."

"Was his name Hanaway?" Carrie asked in quick disbelief.

"Something like that," Dr. Price said absently. He put an arm around them both and gently moved them to the door. "Now, you girls go home. There's no way you can help right now. If there is any change for the better, I'll let you know. If the change is for the worse, I'll send for you."

Carrie went out the door first, numbed by what she had just heard. This couldn't be, she thought. Canning hated Hanaway and would like to do him harm, but he had to have proof.

She heard Neva ask of Dr. Price, "Where is Anna?"

"Asleep in the back room. I gave her some laudanum."

The two girls walked to the waiting surrey and Steve handed them up. As they drove out toward the road, the big black hearse swung into the drive.

Steve turned his head and asked solemnly, "Has Ben passed away?"

Carrie let Neva explain, for her own thoughts were in turmoil. When Neva was finished explaining to Steve, she turned to Carrie. "Do you believe Hanaway shot Ben? I don't and never will."

"I'm going to find out." Carrie leaned forward and said, "Let me off at the courthouse, Steve. I'll walk home from there."

When she entered the courthouse and reached the sheriff's office, she found it locked. The next best source of information would be Hanaway himself. He was not at the hotel. It was then she thought of Harry Hall. His office was locked too. Almost wild with frustration, she walked on home. There she ordered Steve to prowl the streets and courthouse looking for any one of the three men and making an appointment for her with whichever one he found. When by midafternoon Steve had not returned, she and Neva both agreed they needed a nap and went to their rooms.

Now she wakened to Sarita's gentle shake. "Mr. Hall is here to see you, Miss Carrie."

Carrie sat up and stretched. To Sarita's back she said, "If Neva's sleeping, wake her, Sarita, and ask her to come downstairs."

Neva stopped for Carrie on her way, however, and they went downstairs together. They found Hall pacing the library. He halted at sight of them and then moved to meet them. He looked disheveled and worried and tired, Carrie thought.

Hall said, "I'm sorry about Ben, girls. What a hell of an ugly, cruel thing."

Neva nodded and her eyes filled with tears. Carrie said harshly, "Yes." Then in a more gentle voice she said, "Dr. Price said Canning has proof that Hanaway did it."

"Let's talk about that," Hall said grimly, and added, "Why don't we sit down? I've got a lot to tell you."

Carrie and Neva went to the sofa and Hall took the armchair closest to Carrie.

He said, "To begin with, Hanaway's in jail, charged with attempted murder." He recounted Hanaway's and his morning with the sheriff whose evidence against Hanaway was damning enough to jail him.

This afternoon at the preliminary hearing, Hanaway had flat-out accused Dave Reeves of the attempt on Ben's life and the theft of the clerk's receipt to leave at the scene of the murder. Hanaway had pleaded not guilty to the charge of attempted murder. What Hanaway had said had so shaken Kelso's absolute confidence in his case that he had asked the sheriff to bring in Reeves, Hall reported.

"It wound up just as I expected," Hall finished. "The judge set bond at twenty-five thousand dollars. Hanaway can't raise that amount. Neither can I, so he's in jail until the trial."

Carrie looked at Neva, who could have been reading her mind. Carrie looked at Hall. "We can raise it, Harry."

Hall smiled. "That's what I came to ask. I know the court will accept your bank or mine stock for bail money. Nobody can raise that sum in cash."

"Does that mean Hanaway can't leave here?" Carrie asked.

"If Ben lives, Hanaway only has to show up for the trial," Hall said. "Otherwise, he's as free as you are."

Neva said, "If I were Hanaway I'd run, once I was free."

"If you were Hanaway, that's the last thing you'd do," Hall said gently.

They were interrupted by the grinding clang of the doorbell. The girls looked at each other and then Carrie rose and moved swiftly out of the room, almost running. This was news, good or bad, about Ben, she was certain.

She opened the door and saw Dr. Price standing there, a half smile on his long face. "The news is good, Carrie. What I mean is, it isn't bad. I stayed with him until the chloroform wore off and Mrs. Price is feeding him now."

"Is the arm gone?"

"Gone and the bullet dug out."

"Thank God," Carrie said quietly. "Come in, Dr. Price. Come in."

Dr. Price took off his hat, stepped inside, closed the door and said to Carrie's back, "Will you please keep walking until you come to the whiskey, Carrie. I'm in need of some."

XVIII

Hanaway, without handcuffs now that the sheriff was back in the courthouse, was roused from his nap by footfalls on the cellblock stairs. He sat up and watched as Canning stepped down into the corridor and approached his cell, key in hand. He looked tired and in need of a shave. His face as always seemed to hold a barely controlled anger. He unlocked the cell and without even looking at Hanaway, said, "Follow me."

Canning led the way up the stairs and into his office. Carrie, Dr. Price and Hall were standing at the window beside the sheriff's desk. Hanaway said, "Hello, Carrie." Of Hall he asked in puzzlement, "What's this all about, Harry?"

Hall said, "This is Dr. Price, Hanaway."

The doctor took a step forward and he and Hanaway shook hands.

Carrie looked at Hall. "Doesn't he know?"

Hall answered, "No. If I'd told him, he wouldn't have let me go to you."

Hanaway looked from one to the other.

"Know what?" Canning cut in with plain viciousness in his tone of voice, "You're free on bond, Hanaway, only because Ben's alive. Miss Kittrick just posted your bond—twenty-five thousand dollars' worth of bank stock. It doesn't matter if you tried to kill her brother. She feels sorry for you."

"Save the sermon, Wes," Hall said dryly. "Why aren't you out hunting the man that shot Ben?"

"He's right here and you know it," Canning said savagely. He turned to his desk, pulled open a drawer and lifted out Hanaway's gunbelt and handed it to him, saying, "Good hunting, drygulcher."

Facts were coming too fast for Hanaway to under-

105

stand them. After this morning's hearing and the impossibly high bond required to free him, he had resigned himself to months in jail awaiting trial. But Hall had quietly gone to Carrie for the bail money. He looked at Carrie who was watching him with a certain shyness.

"No. I wouldn't have gone to you, Carrie. It wouldn't have been fair, but I guess it's done. One thing I promise you. I won't run," Hanaway said.

"You bet you won't," Canning said sourly. "I'll see to that."

Hanaway strapped on his shellbelt, eyeing Canning. "Don't follow me, Sheriff. If I shot Ben, why wouldn't I shoot you?"

Quiet shock came into Canning's amber eyes, and he did not answer.

"How is Ben?" Hanaway asked.

Dr. Price answered, "I had to take his arm to the shoulder, but he's conscious and eating. I wish I could put some blood in him, but the food will do that."

"Have you seen him, Carrie?" Hanaway asked.

Hall answered for her. "Doc says no, not for a couple of days. Now it's sleep and eat, sleep and eat for Ben."

Hanaway nodded, then looked around him. "I'm tired of this place. Why don't we go?"

Canning said, "Just remember, Hanaway. If Ben dies, I'm after you."

Hanaway regarded him thoughtfully. "That'll take some riding."

"What's that supposed to mean?"

"Why, I'm going to find Reeves and bring him back here. The local sheriff can't and you won't."

He headed for the corridor and the others, except for Canning, followed.

XIX

Hanaway had to wake the hostler sleeping on a cot in the feed stable's office. The man roused, swung his feet to the floor and scratched at his armpit, too bleary with sleep to say anything.

"I'll be gone awhile and I owe money here. Do you know how much?"

"The boss'll know. I don't," the hostler said, his voice sleep-slurred.

Hanaway was silent a moment, then he said, "I'm taking the dun. If I don't show up in a month, the bay belongs to your boss. Fair enough?" At the hostler's nod, he went on, "Tell me where my saddle is and go back to sleep."

Once on the stage road headed north under a chill starlit sky, Hanaway put his mind to the question that had been nagging him since yesterday: where would Reeves go after shooting Ben? Basically, Reeves was a city man and everyone in Kittrick knew that. Would he head back for someplace like Kansas City where he'd be lost in the comings and goings of a transient population? Or would he head West where nobody would know or remember him? Either choice on Reeves's part had to be predicated on the fact that eventually he would be hunted. His planted evidence against Hanaway wouldn't hold up in court; he would be the next suspect and he must run for cover, clever cover. Knowing little of him except that he was shrewd, Hanaway guessed that he would do the contrary thing, the opposite of what was expected of him.

First, though, Hanaway had to prove his hunch that Reeves would never show up to claim his baggage in Junction City.

In midmorning he came to a small adobe crossroads store and corral he remembered from his trip down. It was a stop for the stage that made a team change here. The fresh team was already harnessed and waiting in the corral.

Hanaway dismounted and went into the dark interior of the store. It was a mean and dusty single room with a dirt floor, a deal counter on the left. Behind it were sparsely filled shelves holding staples and dress goods. A bald, middle-aged man in rough work clothes was stretched out on the counter, his head pillowed on a short stack of saddle blankets, his hat lying beside him.

Hanaway moved over to him and the man heard him and swung his feet down and put on his hat.

Hanaway nodded to him. "I'm lookin' for something to eat. Got any canned tomatoes? Crackers?"

The man swung his feet to the other side of the counter, slid down to the floor and reached down a can of tomatoes. He pointed to a barrel resting below a cracked showcase, and said, "Help yourself to the crackers."

Hanaway drew out his knife, opened the blade and began opening the can. He asked, "What do they call this place?"

"Oh, Johnson's, I reckon. I'm Johnson."

Hanaway moved over, took a fistful of crackers from the barrel and then returned to the counter, shaking his head. "No, that wasn't the name. I was supposed to meet a fellow today, but Johnson's don't sound right." He ate a mouthful of the wonderfully cool tomatoes and drank some of the juice. "He would have passed here yesterday morning. Tall, red-haired fellow riding a roan."

Johnson nodded. "He came by yesterday. We talked for a while. He didn't say nothing about meeting anybody, though."

Hanaway ate another chunk of tomato and asked, "Which way'd he head?"

Johnson lifted his hat and with the same hand scratched his bald head. "Well, it was kind of funny."

He pointed to the cracker barrel. "You see that chunk of iron on the dirt by the barrel? Know what it is? It's a railroad car's coupling—or link and pin. He recognized it and asked what in hell it was doing down here so far from the railroad."

Hanaway knew a story was coming and he nodded.

Johnson continued, "I told him I'd been a tracklayer until I couldn't take the sun. I brought that down to remind me. If I ever got a hankering to go back to tracklayin', all I had to do was lift that coupling and I'd get out of the notion."

They both laughed at the story and Johnson continued, "He asked me about construction camps and what they were like. I told him about the ten saloons and whorehouses and gamblers, all of 'em rough."

Hanaway came alert as Johnson next said, "He asked where end of track was now. I told him about the Otterman spur but I couldn't tell him nothing about it because I'd been away from it too long." He paused and asked quietly, "Could your friend be a gambler?"

"That's his business."

"Well, they took plenty away from me before I smartened up. But if he's lived this long, he likely knows his business."

"Which way did he go?" Hanaway asked for a second time.

"He wanted to go West. I talked him out of it." When Hanaway asked why, Johnson replied, "It's rough and it's dry and if you don't know where the water is, you're dead. I told him if he wanted to reach end of steel, he should go north to the Junction and grab a construction train."

"Makes sense," Hanaway said. "You think he's headed there?"

Johnson shrugged. "That's what we talked about."

As Hanaway was finishing his tomatoes, the distant rocketing of horses and the rumble of the stage came to them. He paid up, Johnson pocketed the money and headed out the door for the corral.

Hanaway went out, led his dun out of the shade to the watering trough that lay half in, half out of the pole corral. While his dun drank, Hanaway filled his canteen at the pipe that led from the windmill.

While the stage teams were being changed, he set out north along the stage road. Alone now, he tried to assess what Johnson had told him about his conversation with Reeves. Could Reeves conceivably be heading for the construction camps at the end of steel? If not, why his curiosity? In a way, it made sense for him. Nobody could possibly know or recognize him in that rough tent town that moved every week as the tracks were laid. There wouldn't be any law there because it wasn't even a town. The railroad might halfway police it to protect its property, but it would be teeming with rough men and tough women. Best of all, a gambler could vie with the women and booze for the workers' payroll, and win enough to live.

Or was he just hoping Johnson had unknowingly given him a good steer? Hanaway asked himself. Why, with a good chunk of Ben's money salted away somewhere, wouldn't he take it and head for Mexico or Europe or South America?

And then the answer came to him: *to be near Anna*. If Ben died, she'd come back to him, and they'd go off together. Of course, that was it. The construction train would carry mail back to Junction City and the stage would take his letters to Kittrick and Anna. The trains would also carry the Junction City paper announcing Ben's death if he died, so he could time his letter exactly and safely.

Hanaway arrived in Junction City in late afternoon. After putting up his dun at the feed stable, he headed straight for the railroad depot. There he inquired of the agent if he had sold a ticket to a tall red-haired man within the last twenty-four hours.

"East or west?" the agent asked.

"Either."

The agent shook his head. "Not me, but come around after five when the night agent comes on. Maybe he did."

Hanaway said he would, then crossed the dusty street to the hotel. There he paid for a room and

110

asked that Reeve's trunk and valise he'd sent on ahead yesterday be sent up to his room. After inquiring where the post office was, he went to the hardware store, found the post office in a boarded-off back corner and asked if Dave Reeves had left a forwarding address. The postmaster checked and said he hadn't.

Back at the depot, Hanaway asked the night man the same questions he'd asked the day agent and received a negative answer. Back at the hotel he found that Reeves's trunk and valise had been brought up to his second-floor back room. He pried open both locks with his knife and found just what he'd guessed he'd find—nothing valuable or important or informative. The clothes were a townsman's suits and shoes, assorted shirts, ties and socks, there was nothing written and no letters. Reeves had been careful to pack nothing that would give a hint of where he was bound for or had come from.

Downstairs, Hanaway went into the hotel saloon, found a place at the bar off by himself, and ordered a drink. When it came, he tossed it off quickly, then watered down the second and reviewed the day.

He was certain now that Reeves had bypassed Junction City, to the east or west. All he had to do was pick up the railroad tracks, follow them to the next town, sell his horse, and take a train. It would be a westbound one for sure, Hanaway thought.

What should he himself do? A train would get him to the end of steel quickest but maybe too soon. Reeves should be given time to reach there and set up his game.

But Hanaway knew he was purposely deceiving himself. He wanted to ride his dun to the end of the steel, to travel alone in new and silent country, away from towns and people and talk. There had been too much of all three lately. He wouldn't miss any of it— except for Carrie and Harry Hall.

When he went into the dining room for supper, he knew he would ride.

XX

It took Hanaway an unforgettable week to reach the end of steel. Almost the whole day he traveled the high country with its ponderosa forests where the days were cool, the nights chill. For the most part he lived off the country. Grouse and band-tailed pigeon abounded and took little hunting; he ignored the deer and elk he saw daily who more often just stared at him, then ran.

At a remote lumber mill store he bought a fishing line and hooks and after that he had trout for breakfast each morning. He was rained on every other day and snowed on once and, save for the men at the lumber mill, he never saw another human being. Evenings he camped on the edge of a high mountain park where wild hay was knee-deep to his dun. The heat, the dazzle and the smell of the desert was only a memory, but he knew he'd be returning to it. And to Carrie.

This troubled him more than he liked to admit to himself. Before Ben was shot he could have left with a clear conscience and considerable regret, but now things were changed. The fact that Carrie had gone bond for him put him under an obligation to her. True, she had been under an obligation to him and had only repaid it by saving him from weeks spent in jail, but that very act bound them together even more closely.

He had not found an answer to this even by the day he rode out of the high country and down to the desert floor. Here he kept west until he came to the recently laid railroad tracks, then headed north. The land on both sides of the right of way was scarred and trampled and littered. Hills had been mauled to supply land fill and raw cuts still unrained on slashed through other hills to keep the grade. Everywhere the tent city had been pitched the land had been raped of everything that would burn. It was a vast midden of decaying garbage, cans and bottles, of discarded clothes and boots and broken tools and equipment.

It was dark when Hanaway, riding along the rough worn wagon road that paralleled the rails, came in sight of the construction camp. It sprawled just beyond the base of the slight hill he was on, and he reined in and had his first look. There seemed to be a long street set at right angles to the tract and it bulked with tents set at wide intervals facing tents across the street, a kerosene flare in front of most tents so that the street was almost lit up. He could make out the many boxcars on the temporary siding. There were many lanterns lighted, some moving, some stationary. A strangeness about the sight momentarily puzzled him, and then it came to him. It was the sustained noise that came from the camp. After a week of solitude, its clamor was an assault on the ears, even at a distance.

He put his horse down the hill and was soon traveling alongside a string of boxcars and flatcars and tank cars. As he approached the street, the din of talk grew louder; he came to boxcars in a long row, a lantern lighting their open doors. As he passed one, he caught the fetid stench of unwashed clothes and sweat and alcohol.

The street itself held a throng of workmen milling aimlessly from one tent saloon to another. On most tents the flaps were up and he could see the men crowding the bars, which were planks on sawhorses. There was a similarity about the men he saw that didn't surprise him. Not one was clean-shaven which, considering the way they had to live, was understandable. And every man wore his dusty sweat-stained workclothes and even more dusty hat.

A fist fight started in front of one of the saloons and drew only a small crowd. Hanaway skirted it and slowly rode on. Here were tent stores on one side that sold men's workclothes and boots, a boot-repair tent beside it. Then came a big tent, side flaps up which was jammed with seated gamblers, the drinkers at the bar three deep. Beyond it, and set back from the street, there was another big tent. There was a flare to mark the path to it and a red lantern on a pole by the open door proclaimed its business.

All the while as he rode on there was a restless flow of foot traffic, only an occasional horseman. In a lantern-lit and tiny canvas stall behind a counter loaded with dried fruits and chili peppers, Hanaway saw his first woman, a gray-haired old Mexican crone. A grocery store opposite was stocked with canned staples and flour and cooking utensils, beside a mountain of work gloves.

Altogether, Hanaway thought, this was a town in miniature, under its own pall of dust. A couple of shots rocketed into the night behind him, but nobody seemed to pay attention.

With all this gear to move there must be a wagon yard and corral somewhere and it would be close to the tank cars of water, he thought. He doubted that the railroad would halt its construction traffic to load up the gear of these hangers-on who, in effect, preyed on the construction workers.

He cut north past sleeping tents and dying campfires, crossed ahead of a dead engine and found the corral on the far side of the train. A lantern hung on a pole beside a tent, and the rope corral held many horses. The construction horses would, of course, be held at the very end of steel, ready for the next day's work.

Hanaway dismounted by the metal watering trough and, while his dun drank, he went into the tent. It was more than half filled, ridgerope high, with sacked oats. The front third held a cat and a rocking chair in which an old man sat. He was reading the Bible in the light cast by a lamp on an upended crate beside him. He was wearing half-moon spectacles and now he looked over them at Hanaway's entrance.

"Got room for another horse, my friend?" Hanaway asked.

The old man nodded. "For one night only." He closed his Bible and put it beside the lamp. "Tomorrow, this whole shebang moves up to end of track."

"Me too. Will I see you there?"

"That you will. Throw your saddle in here."

Hanaway went out and took the saddle off the dun. The old man came out with a nosebag of oats, led the dun into the corral, removed his bridle and put on the nosebag. Hanaway pitched his saddle in a corner of the tent, then removed his blanket roll. The old man returned with the bridle and put it beside the saddle.

"You know the gamblers around here, Dad?"

"Too damn well. Why?"

"Know a tall redhead calls himself either Dave or Reeves?"

The old man frowned and thought a moment. "Don't recollect any redhead at all."

Hanaway nodded. "He'd be new. I think I'll take a look around."

"Some people have pulled out already for end of track, even if this is a Saturday night. He could be one of 'em."

Hanaway headed around the train; as he approached the engine he saw a trainman poking around the engine truck with a long-spouted oil can in one hand and a lantern in the other.

"When do you pull out?" Hanaway asked him.

"I blow the whistle at midnight but it still takes another hour to round up the drunks." He shrugged. "That's payday for you."

Minutes later Hanaway understood. The street was thronged with drunken men, as were the gambling tents and stores. Every man seemed to be carrying a bottle in hand or pocket. There were men lying passed out on the street and other men were openly rifling their pockets.

Hanaway had his look at the gambling tents, pushing and shoving through the bedlam until he could come close enough to observe the dealers in the games.

Coming out of the last tent, he was aware that two men had followed him out and trailed him as he headed for the train. When he was certain of it, he stopped and turned close to a flare. They were a rough-looking burly pair and they halted and started to drift apart. Hanaway saw they each had a new axe handle in hand and he took two quick steps backward, his hand driving for his gun. This was the signal for them to charge him. The man on the right lifted his axe handle and, using it as he would a bayonet, lunged at Hanaway. Instead of backpedaling, Hanaway turned sideways, seized the axe handle with his left hand and pulled. Caught charging forward, the man stumbled into the path of his partner who, with ax handle raised high, was also charging.

They crashed together and the first man went sprawling on his face. The second man, with axe handle raised, kept coming. Hanaway shot him in the leg, then stepped out from under the descending axe handle. The man howled with pain, stumbled, tripped on his partner and went down across his legs. Hanaway moved over and kicked the first man in the side of the head, and he simply folded into the dust.

Hanaway holstered his gun, looked around and saw a half dozen drunken onlookers watching this, moved past them and down the noisy street. The pair had probably been a couple of floating riffraff who drifted with the construction camps and knew, from long experience, that payday seldom left a sober man in camp.

Walking back to the corral, Hanaway felt depressed and uncertain. Had he made a wrong guess and followed a sour hunch in thinking Reeves was surely headed for here? Reeves had had time to make it, yet he wasn't here. Had he been here already, heard about the tent town moving tomorrow, and gone on to end of track to await the move? One thing was certain; he must go to end of track to prove his hunch right or wrong.

At the corral, he got his blanket roll from the tent without waking the old man, threw his blankets beside the tent, and rolled into them.

XXI

From the *Junction City Herald*:

Son of a wealthy pioneer who gave his name to a town, country and gold mine. Benjamin Kittrick, aged 37, succumbed to gunshot wounds Saturday. He was ambushed at his ranch home north of Kittrick just a week ago.

Arrested last Sunday for the attempted murder was Hal Hanaway, address unknown. When Kittrick survived the amputation of his right arm and was expected to recover, Hanaway was released from the Kittrick County Jail after posting a $25,000 bond. However, Kittrick passed away in his sleep early Saturday morning. According to the attending physician, Dr. Will Price, death was caused by severe loss of blood.

Hanaway, apparently willing to forfeit bond to escape a murder charge, has disappeared, Sheriff Wesley Canning told this newspaper. An arrest and hold order for Hanaway is being sent to all sheriffs in the territory.

Benjamin Kittrick was president of Kittrick Consolidated gold mines and . . .

Canning tossed the paper onto his desk and swore bitterly. Placing his elbows on the arms of his swivel chair, he steepled his fingers against his shelving chin and regarded the calendar on the wall, not even seeing it. What a damn fool Judge Benson had been to order Hanaway freed on bond. He had, of course, made the bond so high that all of them considered it the equivalent of holding Hanaway in jail. Who could have guessed that the Kittrick girls would bail out the man who shot their brother?

He rose now, took his hat off the hook, put it on and locked the office, then went out the rear corridor door and headed for the wagon shed where his horse was stalled. At Ben's funeral yesterday he had told Harry

Hall to tell Carrie that he wanted to see her today. There was no use putting it off longer.

At the hotel corner he turned his horse up Main Street, rode up it a block, then took the next street, heading toward the Kittricks' house. There was a good reason for this detour. He didn't want to pass Hall's office, for if Hall saw him headed for the Kittricks', he could flag him down and come along. Canning wanted to see Carrie alone.

Sarita answered the door, said Carrie was home, and led him into the library where she left him to find Carrie. Canning, hat in hand, looked around him at the bookshelves. He could not understand why anybody would want so many books, let alone read them. The very sight of a book depressed him, reminding him of the school he had run away from as soon as he could draw puncher's wages.

He heard Carrie come in and turned to her. She looked pale, and her blue eyes seemed overlarge, her face thinned a little.

"Morning, Wes. Harry said you'd call on me today. Sit down, won't you?"

The dress she was wearing was not black, but light blue, and this somehow offended Canning. It was as if Ben, once underground, was no longer mourned, was even forgotten. Canning had already extended his sympathy at the funeral, so that was out of the way.

He walked over to the sofa, waited until Carrie seated herself in the armchair, then sat down, placing his stetson beside him.

"Yes, I told Harry I'd like to talk with you." He hesitated, then added coldly, "About Hanaway."

"Just what about him?"

"I know where he's from. I've already wrote the sheriff up there to be on the lookout for him. You reckon he's headed for there?"

"I think he's headed for Dave Reeves," Carrie said flatly but softly.

"Is that what you'd like to believe or do believe?"

"Oh, both," Carrie said drily.

119

Canning's pale brown eyes regarded her with open derision. "You don't really believe he'll come back here, do you? To face a murder charge, when he's on the high lonesome already?"

"He'll be back, and with Reeves," Carrie said with conviction.

"Well, you've already bet twenty-five thousand on that and lost."

"Have I lost? What's the trial date?"

"It hasn't been set, but me and Kelso will ask for a quick one."

"I'm sure you will, and you'll probably get it," Carrie said. Then she asked, "What are we talking around, Sheriff?"

Canning noted that she had switched from "Wes" to "Sheriff," but that was all right. He said, "I'm going to ask the judge if we can take your forfeited bond money and put it up as reward money for the capture of Hanaway. I never heard of that being done, but still I'm going to ask."

Carrie nodded. "I'll see what Harry Hall says about that."

Canning nodded too. He leaned forward now and asked, "You left my office with Hanaway and Hall. Did he say where he was going?"

"He told you in your office. He was going to find Reeves."

"I know, but where?"

"If I knew, do you really think I'd tell you?"

Canning's amber eyes narrowed. "Not even for Ben's sake?"

Carrie shook her head and said calmly, "You're an impossible man, Sheriff. Simple-minded too."

Canning said angrily, "All right. I'll bring them both back. Would that suit you?" At Carrie's nod of assent, he said, "Then where was Hanaway headed?"

"Reeves sent a trunk to Junction City. He paid the stage driver to leave it at the hotel there. Hanaway was going to check there first, but he didn't think Reeves was ever going to claim it. He thought . . ."

"I know what he thought," Canning cut in. "Hall

120

told the judge at the hearing. What I want to know is where Hanaway was headed after Junction City."

"He didn't know, so how could I know?"

"You can't even guess, I reckon."

"You reckon right, Sheriff," Carrie said.

Canning picked up his hat and rose. His face flushed at the thought of what he was about to ask, but he plunged ahead. "Is Ben's—ugh—lady friend still at Diamond K?"

Carrie rose too. "So far as I know."

"Thank you," Canning said stiffly, then added, "I meant what I said. I'll bring them both back."

He let himself out, swearing under his breath. How in hell could he bring them back if he couldn't find them? Maybe Anna Reeves could help. As he mounted he tried to recall what that wild-eyed Hall had said at the preliminary hearing. Ben had been killed by Reeves because he'd been fired from a good job, Hall said, and because Ben had taken Anna, who wasn't his sister, away from him. Canning didn't believe him, but Ben was the only man who could prove Hall a liar and he was dead. Still, Anna Reeves should be questioned, cunningly if possible.

It was a blasting hot day and by the time Canning reached Diamond K his shirt was sweat-plastered to his back and the hair at the back of his head was dripping sweat onto his shirt collar.

Answering the door, Lupe asked him in and then went to fetch Anna. The last time he was in this house Anna Reeves had been too hysterical to question; he did get out of her, before Dr. Price drugged her, that she hadn't been in the room when Ben was shot and saw nothing except his shattered body.

When she came into the room from the bedroom wing, she was wearing the same black dress she had worn yesterday at the funeral, and it made her pale hair seem almost white. She gave him a sad but beautiful smile, waved him to an armchair and sat down, saying, "It's a hot day to be riding, Sheriff. You must have some important business."

She was so beautiful that Canning could only stare

at her. Where Carrie had looked almost haggard, Anna looked rested and only reserved, he thought.

He shook his head and said, "Nothing important, but maybe you can help me."

"If I can, surely."

"Well, that damned Hanaway—excuse me—has jumped the country, looks like. Leastways, he's not around."

Anna looked puzzled. "You think I know where he is? How could I and why would I?"

Canning raised his hands, palms out and said, "No, no. Nothing like that. It's just that he told Carrie Kittrick he was going to hunt down Reeves." He paused, lowering his hands. "Would you know where your brother is?"

"Why, the day he left he said he was heading for California to see our brother," Anna said.

"He stopped by that day, then?"

"Of course. To say goodbye."

"Did Hanaway know that?" Canning asked.

"I'm sure I don't know, Sheriff. What does Hanaway want with my brother?"

Canning grimaced. "He thinks he killed Ben."

"And you believe him?" Anna asked incredulously.

Canning shook his head. "No, you've got me wrong again. I figure that if Hanaway knows where your brother is, that's where I look for Hanaway with a warrant. But I don't think he's headed for California." He frowned. "Where is your older brother in California?"

"We write him care of Wells Fargo in San Francisco. I don't think Hanaway could possibly find Dave with that little to go on, even if he knows where to look."

"You're right. I don't either," Canning said gloomily. He rose and asked, "Is Dave sending for you?"

Anna nodded. "As soon as he finds George."

"Well, thanks. I think Hanaway's gone for good, but I've got to try and find him."

Anna rose and said, "Good hunting."

When the sheriff was gone, Anna went back to her

bedroom. It held a huge bed and wardrobe and the floor was carpeted by a big rose-flowered rug. Anna moved over to the far corner of the rug, lifted it and picked up an envelope from the floor. From it she took out a letter, which read:

April 2

Dearest: I hear Ben was shot and killed. Now that you are free and broke, why don't we throw in together again? I have money for both of us, and we'll make more. Buy a ticket in Junction City for Indian Bend. Stop there. My name here is C.D. Williams, so write and address End of Track, North. Like always, love.

DAVE

Anna had kept the letter hidden from Lupe whom she assumed, but couldn't prove, read all her mail.

The heart of the matter was this: Dave's letter was dated April 2. Ben had died April 7. How did Dave, five days ahead of Ben's death, know that he was dead? Because Dave had shot him, of course.

She felt some bitterness toward Dave, for in killing Ben, Dave had robbed her of a fortune. She didn't wholly blame him, because Ben had bought her away from him. But the nicest part of this, the very nicest, was that Dave had a large chunk of Ben's money. Dave had, in effect, rented her to Ben for a year, and she considered herself well paid.

She reread the letter, memorizing it, moved over to the fireplace, took a match from a dish on the mantel and was about to strike it and burn the letter when she reconsidered. Dangerous as it was to keep it, she decided she would, for it was a lever on Dave she could use in the future.

XXII

Hanaway reached end of track in midmorning. On the way here, following the track, he had seen two dead men on the right of way, vultures feeding on them. Both probably had been pitched out of the construction boxcars in the night. Lack of any law here and the anonymity of the construction workers made for heedless deaths and few burials, for nobody cared about a stranger who probably deserved his killing.

The end of track was a dreary makeshift which would be compounded when the saloons, stores and whores arrived later in the day. With no plan whatsoever, the plain on both sides of the track was dotted with tents of every size and description, with the bunk tents predominant. There was a huge boarding tent where the workers were fed their two daily meals at daybreak and nightfall. The hundreds of horses and mules were tied at the long V-shaped wooden hayricks which would be filled again with wild hay when the stock was working. A couple of acres beside the windmill and its big excavated pond were set aside for the scrapers and harness.

Hanaway let his horse drink his fill at the pond, then went in search of information. The workers, some still drunk from last night, were milling aimlessly around on their free day, visiting or playing cards, or even singing.

At the very end of track past the long line of flatcars of rails and ties he came to a tent whose side held the legend Grading Boss painted in faded black letters. Beyond it, four plowed furrows stretched as far as the eye could see on either side of where the track would be laid. Tomorrow, the scrapers by the dozens with their teams would crisscross these furrows, scraping up the loose earth to build up the grade for the ties and rails.

The fly of the tent was open and Hanaway dismounted and went inside. A man seated on a campstool was doing some paperwork at a deal table. He was a bald man, wearing steel-rimmed glasses, and his heavy face was scarred by many, long-forgotten fights.

He looked up at Hanaway, and he was scowling.

"There's no place to knock," Hanaway said mildly. "Sorry to bother you, but maybe you could help me."

Surprisingly the grade boss smiled. "Well, Sunday is the day to ask for help from above. What can I do for you here below?"

Hanaway smiled too. "I'm looking for a professional gambler. Tall, red-haired, thirty-odd, with kind of a weasel face. Can't have been here long."

The grade boss regarded him with amusement. "You out to save his soul on this fine Sunday?"

"I don't reckon he has a soul to save, so the answer is no."

The grade boss thought a moment, then shook his head. "Tell you what. You passed the boarding tent on your way here. Go back to it and ask for Morgan, the boarding boss. He works all day for money to gamble with all night. He'd know about every game in camp."

Hanaway thanked him and started back for the boarding tent. It was a vast open-sided affair containing trestle tables and facing benches. The kitchen wing with its huge black iron ranges and meat-cutting blocks was where he found Morgan giving orders to a half dozen bull cooks.

He was a cadaverous man so tall that his bloodshot eyes were on a level with Hanaway's. He listened carefully to Hanaway's description of Reeves and when Hanaway was finished, nodded his head. "You must mean Seedy."

"Seedy?"

"He's C.D. Williams but everybody calls him Seedy. Set up about three-four days ago. Got a couple of fellows on the other games, but he handles the poker. They're a rough bunch, so watch yourself. Got a red-striped tent so you can't miss it."

Hanaway thanked him and headed for his horse. This Williams had to be Reeves; he answered to his description and the timing fit. In the eight days Hanaway had been riding here, Reeves, taking the train, must have rounded up an outfit and dealers and brought them to the end of track. He had the money to buy the games and pay his dealers.

Locating Reeves was one thing, but getting him back to Kittrick was another, Hanaway knew. He had no power of arrest and Dave would fight the return to Kittrick. Even if he was successfully returned there, Canning would very likely refuse to charge him and would probably free him.

The only thing he could do, Hanaway thought, was to take one thing at a time. Once he had him, should he ride back with him the way he had come? That would mean keeping Reeves tied up day and night, and he knew from past experience how exhausting and dangerous that could be. Accident to man or horse could mean doubling up on one horse. Not even his dun, strong as he was, could take many days of that. If they didn't double up and Reeves was forced to walk, Hanaway knew Reeves wouldn't make it, for he wouldn't have the stamina. No, the train was a far better bet—if he was allowed to take it.

As he rode through the busy street he saw that the vanguard of wagons and pack horses from the old camp were arriving. Tents were being set up and wagons unloaded and others would trickle in for the rest of the day. Well back from the tracks and past the loafing, drinking or strolling workers, Hanaway picked out Reeves's red-striped tent, but he did not go close to it, since Reeves might spot him and immediately be put on his guard.

Of a trainman walking alongside the cars, Hanaway asked where the trainmaster could be found and was told to look in the crummy on the far siding for a man called Ryan. There he found a middle-aged, potbellied man in shirtsleeves reading a newspaper. He reined in, the man looked up and they both nodded. "I'm looking for a man called Ryan, the trainmaster."

"That's me." He folded his newspaper held in a fist and, elbows on knees and arm extended, regarded Hanaway. "Anything botherin' *you*?"

Hanaway smiled. "I reckon you could say that." He swung out of the saddle, came up to the steps and the dun followed him.

"Nice-lookin' horse. Looks like a stayer, too." His glance shifted from the dun to Hanaway. "What's your trouble?"

"That horse, mostly, and another fellow. We all got to get to Kittrick in a hurry. I hear around you don't sell tickets and take freight yet."

"Not from Indian Bend to end of track. But we go back empty. You lookin' for a ride?"

"If that's possible." He took out an eagle from his pocket and showed it in his palm. "Would that cover it?"

Ryan looked at the coin, then raised his surprised glance to Hanaway's face. "Hell, twice over."

Hanaway gestured to the caboose. "Can I have a look in there? I've never seen one."

Ryan rose and led the way into the caboose. Two benches faced a small table fastened to the car's side. There was an iron ladder beyond that lifting to the cupola, a double-deck bunk opposite, a flat iron stove anchored to the floor, a pile of wood, a rack of lanterns on the right wall, and a water bucket on a counter that held the sink.

Hanaway extended the eagle, asking, "Can we ride in this?"

The trainmaster accepted the eagle, saying, "Ain't supposed to, but who'll know?"

"That extra money is for you." He pointed to the bunk supports. "I want to tie a man to that brace."

Ryan studied him, then asked, "You a lawman?"

"No. I'll be taking this man to a lawman, though."

"What's he done?"

"Tried to kill a man and blame it on me."

127

Oddly, Ryan smiled. "And you don't like that."

Hanaway nodded and the trainmaster thought a moment. Finally he said, "Well, there ain't any kind of law here at the end of the track and God knows it needs some. If you're doin' the law's job and they ain't, I guess it's up to us to help. Sure, bring him here."

"What time do we leave?" Hanaway asked.

"Midnight. We'll haul out a string of empties. After supper we can load your horse on a car that's waiting at the chute—unless you'll be needing him."

"No. I'll have him here. Much obliged."

Ryan watched him ride off. As soon as Hanaway was out of sight he reached for the newspaper in his hip pocket that he had rammed there after Hanaway rode up. It was a copy of the *Junction City Herald* and its banner line read: BEN KITTRICK MURDERED.

He reread the story with new interest now. Finished, he was certain he had just been talking with Hal Hanaway. He was equally certain that Hanaway was not jumping his bond, for he'd said he wanted to be in Kittrick as soon as possible. Did Hanaway know that Ben Kittrick had died and that he was wanted for his murder by all county sheriffs in the territory? Ryan thought not, for hadn't Hanaway said, "He *tried* to kill a man and blame it on me?"

In his mind Ryan went over the entire conversation with Hanaway. The man hadn't given his name because in this country you seldom gave your name and never asked a man his, so there was nothing strange about that.

Summing up his own feelings, Ryan decided he liked the man. He would have helped him without being rewarded and before he knew who Hanaway was. And, in good time, he must tell him of the danger he was walking into.

Hanaway tied his horse to the hayrick to feed among construction teams, crawled between two freight cars and was in the moving camp again. Here and there the tents were going up with the aid of helpful construction workers.

It was the same scene as last night, only enormously enlarged by the bunk tents and more men, some of them as drunk as they'd been then.

Roaming among the tents, he came to a small half tent that was tended by the same old Mexican crone he had seen last night. He bought a handful of enchiladas and some grapes from her and then had a stand-up meal of the fiery enchiladas which he tried to cool down with the grapes. Afterward he roamed the camp again until he found what he was looking for— a place where he could watch Reeves's tent without being seen.

It was the supper bell that brought Reeves and two companions out of the tent. They headed for the boarding tent and Hanaway, well screened by tents, watched them.

Reeves was dressed for the part of a gambler with long-tailed black coat, shirt and cuffs with ruffles and a black string tie. He moved among the roughly dressed construction workers with a certain disdain, and because of his two rough-looking companions who were both packing pistols, there was no derision in the greetings he received on his way to the boarding tent.

Hanaway knew that between now and midnight he had to figure some way to separate Reeves from the two men he supposed were Reeves's dealers. When the three men were lost in the crowd moving toward supper, Hanaway headed for Reeves's striped tent. He was certain that the tent with its gambling money would be guarded. As he approached, he was in the dusk that the kerosene flare in front of the tent's open flaps lighted against the coming night. He went past the flaps and halted, looking about him. Behind the small bar with no bottles visible, sat a burly-looking guard with a shotgun lying within reach on the bar top. As Hanaway took in the faro layout and two big poker tables, he noted a canvas-covered doorway cut in the back of the tent. When he looked back at the guard, the man had his hand resting on the shotgun.

"You closed down?" Hanaway asked.

"No. Come back after supper," the guard said. "You want to make some money, this is the place."

Hanaway nodded, turned and went out into the lowering darkness. Flares and lamps were being lighted all over the camp and the bunk tents began to glow softly as lanterns were lit inside. Remembering the canvas door at the rear of Reeves's tent, Hanaway made a half circle of the big tent, careful to avoid the guy ropes. At the rear of the big tent there was a small wall tent; this was where the canvas door obviously led, and where Reeves and his crew probably slept. Sizing up the wall tent, Hanaway was certain that while the tent could house four men, Reeves would want his privacy.

Lying on his belly, he lifted up the taut canvas far enough to see inside. He had been right. In the dim and fading light, Hanaway could make out a single cot, a closed trunk at its head. Bowl and pitcher sat on a crate across from the cot, and beside the crate, spread out on clean canvas, was a pile of clean shirts and a couple of jackets.

Rising to his feet, Hanaway was fairly sure that this was Reeves's quarters. The trunk close to his pillow very likely had a padlock and would be chained to the cot, for this would be where Reeves kept his gambling money.

Heading for the railroad tracks now by a route that skirted the big noisy boarding tent, Hanaway sought out the trainmaster's caboose. There was a lamp lighted inside but Ryan was not yet back from supper. Hanaway seated himself on the top step where he had found Ryan sitting earlier and stared into the night. He wondered how he was going to capture Reeves. Undoubtedly Reeves's crew had pitched their tents close enough to Reeves's tent so that they could hear and answer a call for help. Besides, with the work train leaving for Indian Bend at midnight, what assurance was there that Reeves wouldn't be running his

games at that hour surrounded by a bunch of drunk-
en workers of the grading crew?

His thoughts were interrupted by the approach of a
man carrying a lantern; Hanaway saw that it was
Ryan. The trainmaster halted at the foot of the steps
and said, "Get enough to eat?"

"More than enough," Hanaway answered.

"Well, let's go load your horse."

Hanaway joined him and they moved down the
string of cars until they came to the corral loading
chute. While Ryan opened the corral gate and
tramped up the chute to open the door of the boxcar,
Hanaway circled the pond and untied his horse, let
him drink, then led him into the corral and up the
chute into the empty car where Ryan was waiting
with a lantern.

The interior of the car held many stalls for the safe
transport of fresh construction teams to the end of the
track. Hanaway unsaddled, tied his dun in a stall
whose manger was half full of hay, took the lariat off
his saddle, gave his dun an affectionate slap on the
rump and left the car. Ryan, following, slid the door
closed and followed Hanaway out of the corral. As
Ryan was closing the corral gate, he said, "I bet that
horse is wondering what the hell is happening. Ever
shipped him before?"

"No, but he'll be all right," Hanaway said.

Together they walked back to the caboose and
Ryan led the way into it, put the lantern on the table
and sat down. He gestured to the seat opposite and
said, "Figured out how you'll get your man?"

"Sort of," Hanaway said wryly. He put his lariat on
the bench. "Tell me, do these gambling tents stay
open late on a Sunday night?"

"That they do and so do the men. Some of them
will show up drunk in the morning and be fired. We
ought to care but we don't because there are fifty
men loafing around camp without work, so we put
them on in place of the drunks."

"Then that means my man will likely be dealing
poker when the train pulls out?"

Ryan nodded. "Unless you can toll him out before that."

That, Hanaway thought, would take some doing. He thought he had a way of getting to Reeves without having to deal with his companions, but it was risky at best. He judged that Reeves would be dealing from a chair at the poker table closest to the canvas door to his tent so as to make sure nobody entered the tent. He would be close enough to his trunk to hear if anybody tried to break into it. At least, Hanaway thought, that's where I would sit if I were in his place.

He said to Ryan as he rose, "You'll want some sleep before you pull out of here. If I'm not here before midnight, can you unload my horse at Indian Bend and put him up at a feed stable?"

Ryan nodded and said quietly, "I reckon you'll show up in time."

Hanaway pointed to his lariat on the bench. "I'll leave that here. Will your engineer whistle before he takes off?"

"I'll tell him to and then wait five more minutes." Ryan said. "Good luck and take care, my friend."

Hanaway nodded, then started for the door, slowly halted and turned to face Ryan. He asked curiously, "Why is midnight the time you pull out?"

Ryan frowned, then shrugged. "No real reason. We're supposed to meet the early train at Indian Bend and help with the switching."

"So you can't leave later than midnight—but can you leave earlier?"

A look of surprise came on Ryan's face. "Why yes, we could. I'm trainmaster so its up to me. Why?"

"Well, I don't know what I'll be pulling down on my head," Hanaway answered. "If I get my man, there'll be at least three men hunting the camp for him. Sooner or later they'll think of the train and come to search it."

Ryan nodded. "I can see that. What you're saying is, you want us to pull out as soon as you get your man, but no later than midnight." At Hanaway's nod,

Ryan continued, "The fireman will be firing up about now. I can tell him to hurry it. The engineer is likely sleeping, he beds down in the car behind the tender. All he's got to do when I wake him is pull on his boots."

Hanaway smiled. "Much obliged. The reason I asked is that if I miss him on the first try, I'll have to try again."

Ryan rose, took the lantern, passed Hanaway, swung down the steps and halted. When Hanaway was beside him, Ryan said, "Give us an hour to get steam up. Take care now."

Hanaway waited until his eyes became adjusted to the darkness, then crossed the tracks and moved into the camp. It was still thronged with men who would have to be up at daylight. A few of the bunk tents were dark but not many. He had a useless hour to kill before Ryan's fireman got up a head of steam. The boarding tent was still serving, he noticed.

At a newly pitched tent saloon he shouldered through to the bar, bought himself a half glass of whiskey, drank it slowly, them went back to the boarding tent and ate a meal of mostly cold food. Afterward he cruised the camp. It seemed to him that every store and saloon he'd seen last night was now in business here, including the tent with the red lantern hanging beside its open flaps. There were, of course, many dogs running loose in the camp and he supposed that the workers, womanless and without families, picked up a dog as a substitute for the affection of humans. Some of the drifters with few possessions save a blanket were already stretched out sleeping after their ten-mile hike from the old camp.

When he judged an hour had passed, he headed for Reeves's gambling tent. Pausing in the doorway, he saw that the tent was crowded with drinkers, gamblers and men watching the games. Moving into the crowd until he could see at the poker table, he got a glimpse of Reeves's red hair. As Hanaway expected, Reeves was seated in a chair just in front of the canvas door. Hanaway moved outside and made a half circle in the darkness. There was a lantern burning in Reeves's tent but no shadows against the canvas. However, to make sure it was empty, Hanaway did what he had done earlier—lay on his belly and looked under the canvas. Nobody was in the tent.

Rising again, he drew out his heavy knife from the pocket of his duck jacket, opened it and slit the canvas from the ridgerope to the ground. Once inside he moved over to the lamp, memorized the interior of the tent, then blew out the lamp.

Knife still in hand, he backtracked most of his half circle, passing three guy ropes on his way. At the first he halted and cut the guy rope, then raced for the second and swiftly cut that too. The third was more stubborn but he cut through it. By this time, as the tent began to sag toward its center pole, there were shouts of alarm and warning from inside the tent. Hanaway raced back to Reeves's tent, moved toward the canvas door, drew his gun and stood beside the door, back to canvas.

Inside the big tent there was pandemonium. He could hear shouts of "Brace that pole!" "Blow the lamp!" "God, we'll smother." The tent door began to sag and now Hanaway heard Reeves's voice close to him yelling, "Bernie, Sam! Outside, outside! Get the ropes!" The air from the collapsing tent lifted the curtain. Suddenly there was a wavering shadow cast in the tent doorway and then the canvas was yanked aside as Reeves ran through the doorway. Just inside the tent he halted, looking toward the unlit lamp.

Without a word of warning, without a sound of movement Hanaway lifted his gun and wapped Reeves across the skull with the barrel of his six gun. Reeves's knees bent and he was falling when Hanaway caught him. Hanaway holstered his gun, knelt before Reeves, loosened his hold and Reeves fell over his shoulder. Rising now, Hanaway distributed Reeves's weight more comfortably, then moved through the slit tent—back out into the night. From the sounds he heard, men seemed to be milling at the big tent's door. He cast a glance over his shoulder and saw that half the tent was still up but sagging, the other half collapsed.

As he headed for the tracks, Hanaway heard voices yelling, "Fire! Fire!" Again he looked back and saw that part of the tent was in flames. Probably one of the lanterns over the gambling tables had spilt over as the tent collapsed and set the canvas on fire, Hanaway judged.

As he made his way to the tracks, a man passed him running toward the burning tent. It was not an unusual sight in this camp to see a man carrying another; it was usually a case of a man helping a drunken passed-out friend. To make it appear that way, Hanaway walked with an uneven lurch. All the men he met were running the other way, for if the fire were not put out, it could spread to the other tents and get out of control.

As he neared the tracks he saw to his amazement and delight that the engine had traveled the Y. As he approached, the engine began to move and the long line of freight cars clanked into motion. Hanaway stopped, puzzled, and then realized that the engineer would pull the string of cars past the Y and then back into it to pick up his caboose.

He let the cars pull past him, then headed for the caboose where the lamp was lit. Now he could see Ryan standing at the switch down the tracks, lantern in hand.

Hanaway climbed the caboose steps, went inside, knelt by the lower bunk and rolled the still unconscious Reeves onto its blanket-covered mattress. He rose then and hauled and tugged at Reeves until he lay on his belly. Afterward Hanaway picked up his lariat from the bench, uncoiled it and tied Reeves's hands behind his back. With the remaining length of the rope he tied Reeves's feet together and finally anchored the lariat to the bunk post. Hanaway knew that in this position Reeves could not use his hands to free his feet.

Hanaway next grabbed Reeves's red hair and turned his head to face the aisle. Then he searched

Reeves's clothes and found a derringer in his coat pocket. Afterward he was glad to slide into one of the benches and wait for his labored breathing to subside.

He judged it was only a couple of minutes after he sat down that he heard the clank of the approaching cars. There was a not so gentle bump, then he heard Ryan put the pin in the link of the coupling. Ryan didn't signal with his lantern but climbed the caboose steps and halted just inside the open door. He looked at Reeves and shifted his glance to Hanaway and smiled. "That's pretty good timing, Hanaway," Ryan said.

Hanaway didn't recall having told Ryan his name and he said, "How do you know my name's Hanaway?"

Ryan pulled a copy of his *Junction City Herald* out of his hip pocket and tossed it on the table. "Reckon you ought to read that before you hit Indian Bend. Unless you want me here, I'll ride up front with the boys."

"Don't need you, Ryan. Thank your crew for me and save a hell of a lot of those thanks for yourself. I'm obliged."

Ryan nodded. "I'll shut the door against these cinders. See you later, Hanaway."

Hanaway unfolded the newspaper and when he read the headline he felt a pang of anguish. It was for Carrie and Neva. Ben would be buried by now and they were alone.

When he finished reading the whole story, he knew why Ryan had shown the paper to him. He was a hunted man now and according to the last line of the *Herald's* story there was $10,000 head money for apprehension of him dead or alive; the money was posted by the Kittrick County Commissioners. It was interesting to consider how he'd get Reeves from Indian Bend to Kittrick; he'd have to give it some thought. He glanced over the paper at Reeves and saw that his eyes were open watching him and that they were filled with purest malice. Reeves cleared his throat and asked, in a voice made ragged by anger, "What do you want with me, Hanaway?"

"You already know," Hanaway answered.

"I don't owe you anything and never did! Untie me, goddamnit."

"All you owe me is your left. I think a jury will say so too." He watched Reeves a moment and then asked, "Read the last *Junction City Herald?*"

When Reeves shook his head, Hanaway straightened the paper and read the banner aloud as he watched for some reaction in Reeves's face. It was scowling and his eyes were wary.

Then Hanaway read the story aloud in its entirety. When he was finished, Reeves was silent for many moments and then he asked Hanaway, "Why did you kill Ben? What did he ever do to you?"

Hanaway only shook his head. "It's got to be better than that, Reeves. Want to try again?"

"What in hell do you want me to say?" Reeves exploded.

"Only what you'll say in the long run—that you killed Ben."

"How could I have?" Reeves demanded. "If that paper's right, I left Kittrick for here the morning of the night Ben was shot."

"And you were headed for end of track then?"

"Of course I was. I've been a gambler and never denied it. Why wouldn't I head for where the construction money is?"

"Why didn't you pick up your trunk at Junction City?"

"Why, once I was settled I was going to send for it."

"No. You were going to leave it," Hanaway said. "You thought you'd killed Ben with that shot. Even with the planted evidence against me that Canning found, you weren't taking any chances. You wanted to cover your back trail so you didn't even show in Junction City."

"Who says that?"

"I do. I claimed your trunk and opened it and searched it."

"I don't know what you're talking about," Reeves said sullenly.

"If you weren't on the run, why did you change your name to C. D. Williams at end of track?"

"Who says I did?"

"You should have taken the trouble to dye your hair," Hanaway said quietly. "There's not too many tall, red-haired gamblers. But you took the long chance, didn't you?"

Reeves didn't answer. He tried to turn on his back and could not. Hanaway rose, braced himself against the sway of the train, which was going at a good clip now, and went over to the water bucket. Afterward he took a dipper of water back to Reeves, who only shook his head and refused to accept a drink. Hanaway went back to his seat then and saw that Reeves had closed his eyes. Hanaway knew there would be more conversation before they reached Indian Bend. Right now, Hanaway guessed, Reeves was assessing the information Hanaway had passed on from the newspaper. Very likely he was pondering the same question Hanaway was—how was Hanaway going to get from Indian Bend to Kittrick?

Hanaway was reading the rest of the paper for want of something better to do when Reeves's voice cut in on him. "You've got a price on your head, haven't you?"

Without looking up from his paper, Hanaway nodded. "How you going to get me through Indian Bend and Junction City? You can't gag and tie me, all I've got to do is to yell 'This man's Hanaway.' Like that?"

Still Hanaway didn't look up from his paper, but he answered, "I was thinking of cutting your throat."

"Be funny," Reeves said.

This time Hanaway looked at him. "I don't think you'll open your mouth in either of those towns, because if you do I'll shoot you. You forget I'm already

138

wanted for killing a man. What's one more, especially you?"

Reeves held his glance for many long moments, then he said, "If you're to try to prove you're innocent, you'll need me alive. You won't shoot me." .

"You're a gambler," Hanaway said. "Want to bet your life on that?"

XXIII

By the time Sheriff Canning was through arguing with the Kittrick County Commissioners, the late morning stage for Junction City had already left. He went back to his office in a sour and combative mood. His request of the Commissioners that the twenty-five-thousand-dollar bail money, forfeited by Hanaway, be applied to a reward of the same amount for the capture of Hanaway, had been refused by the commissioners. They had argued that a reward of this staggering amount would turn the whole territory into a gang of bounty hunters. Sedentary men would leave their jobs and die in the desert. Strangers to the country would come in and die likewise. It would be the California Gold Rush of 1849 all over again. They suggested a reward of five thousand dollars, which, God knows, was a fortune in this country.

Canning's argument that the more men hunting for Hanaway the better chance there was of finding him was acknowledged. They compromised on a reward of ten thousand dollars which did fitting honor to Ben Kittrick and would most certainly alert all the law officers in the territory.

One argument settled, another started. Canning wanted to know if he would be eligible for the reward if he caught Hanaway. The commissioners said no, that was his job. Then Canning said he hadn't had a vacation in three years and was taking one. Marshal Barnard could be named acting sheriff. If Canning, on vacation, caught Hanaway, could he collect the reward? the sheriff asked. After an hour's wrangling between him and the commissioners, it was voted he could.

It wasn't all he wanted, Canning thought, but it

was a substantial part of it. Now he leaned back in his swivel chair and sighed. If he lingered any longer in town, people would be wondering why he wasn't on Hanaway's trail, so he'd have to ride out of town publicly to reassure voters that he was doing his job. The trouble was, he thought gloomily, he had no notion of where to start looking for Hanaway. Working on the theory that Hanaway would be searching for Reeves, then the only thing he could do was hunt down Reeves. Since many people saw Reeves's trunk loaded on the stage for Junction City, then that railroad town was the place to pick up the trail. Besides, Junction City had the closest press where the reward posters could be printed.

The sheriff reached for a clean piece of paper, took up his pen and printed this message:

ON VAKATION HUNTING HANAWAY
SEE MARSHEL BARNARD

SHERIFF WES CANNING

He hunted through his desk drawers for a nail, found one, then went over to the door and nailed the message on it. Afterward he reached under the cot in the corner and drew out a blanket roll which he kept there for emergencies requiring quick action.

Locking the door, now he reread his sign, then headed out the side door for the shelter where his horse was stalled. Before passing through town, he left word at the feed stable that he was headed for Junction City and wouldn't be gone longer than three weeks.

When Canning rode past the Diamond K his gloom deepened as he looked at the house. Anna Reeves had said Dave was headed for California and he wondered if Hanaway knew that. Once Hanaway learned of Ben's death and that he was a wanted man, there was no reason at all for him to stay in this country. In fact, there was every reason why he shouldn't if he wanted to save his neck.

Later, Canning watered his horse at the trough by

141

Johnson's store. He dismounted and stretched his legs, but saw no need for talking with Johnson.

It was past suppertime when he rode into Junction City, put up his horse at the feed stable and then with his bandy-legged swagger headed for the hotel. Of the middle-aged desk clerk he inquired, "Has a tall, red-haired man calling himself Dave Reeves registered here during the last ten days?"

"Reeves," the clerk mused. "Why yes, he took a room and had his trunk sent up. I remember him because he walked out and left the trunk in his room." The clerk frowned. "You said red-haired. This man wasn't a redhead. Tall, dark-haired he was, with gray eyes."

Hanaway, Canning thought.

"You wouldn't know how he got out of here? I mean, did he ride out on a horse or did he take the train?"

"I can't answer that," the clerk said. "Why don't you ask the night agent over at the depot?"

Canning was hungry, but he wanted to talk to the agent first. At the depot he saw that Emory was on night duty. He knew him and they shook hands and asked about each other. When that was over, Canning asked his question. "This could be about ten days ago, but do you remember a tall fella' coming in here? About thirty, cowboy clothes, gray eyes, dark hair? Did he buy a ticket?"

Emory frowned and said, "I don't recollect, Sheriff."

"All right. Here's another question. Did a tall red-haired, blue-eyed fella dressed in cowboy clothes come in and buy a ticket east or west?"

The agent's jaw slackened and he said, "Now I remember. The fella you described first came in and asked the question you just did. Had I sold a ticket to a tall red-haired fella. I hadn't seen the redhead."

That's Hanaway, on Reeves's trail, Canning thought.

"Much obliged, Emory. Take care of yourself, hear?"

Canning was even hungrier now but he crossed the road and found the newspaper office a block down the street. The door was locked, but keeping his hands on either side of his eyes, he looked through the window past the counter and desk and saw a printer working at the composing stone under an overhead lamp.

Moving over to the door, Canning tried the knob. The door was locked. He rattled the door and the printer looked up, moved toward the street, and opened the door. Canning reached in his hip pocket, drew out the crumpled paper containing the text of the reward dodger on Hanaway and extended it to the lanky, inky-fingered printer. Canning could smell the booze on the printer's breath as the man unfolded the paper and read the text.

"Two hundred copies. Send 'em to Marshal Barnard in Kittrick." He paused, waiting for the printer to finish reading, then he added, "Better give that to someone that can spell."

The printer looked at him and said, "You don't want a speller, you want a translator."

Canning flushed. "You can tell what I want there. Write it any way you damn please, but get it done quick."

He turned and headed back for the hotel. There he had a fast drink in the bar, then went into the almost empty dining room and ordered his supper. After he had wolfed it down and was on his second cup of coffee he reviewed the information he had picked up here.

That damn Hanaway rode in here, pretended he was Reeves, searched the trunk, asked about Reeves at the depot and got no information, then rode out. To where? Which direction? Did anything in Reeves's trunk hold any information as to where Reeves was headed? I'd better look at that trunk, Canning thought.

He left the dining room, paid for his supper at the desk, then said to the clerk, "Where'll I find the trunk this fella left in his room?"

"I'll show you." The clerk came from behind the desk, crossed the small lobby to a door set in the back wall. Opening it, he said to Canning, "Better wait here until I light a lamp."

He vanished down the stairs into darkness. Presently lamplight bloomed in the darkness and Canning descended the stairs into a big storeroom. The clerk was standing under a wall lamp. He pointed to a trunk and valise, said, "That's them. Blow the lamp when you're done," and went back up the stairs.

As he had expected, Canning found nothing in the trunkful of clothes that would indicate where Reeves was headed.

If there had been any letters that gave a clue, Hanaway probably had them. He closed the trunk, blew the lamp, climbed the stairs, crossed the lobby and halted on the boardwalk in the lowering dusk.

All right, Canning thought with bulldog stubbornness, he didn't take the train, he rode out, so let's find out which way. At the feed stable, he found the bucktoothed young hostler lying on the sagging cot in the tiny shack office of the feed barn. A lamp was lighted against coming darkness. The young hostler sat up, swung his feet to the floor and asked, almost unbelievingly, "You riding back tonight, Sheriff?"

"No. I just wanted to talk with you." The sheriff moved over to the desk and sat on the edge of it. "This was almost ten days ago, I reckon. See if you remember this man. He put his horse up here." He described Hanaway while the hostler listened carefully. When he was finished, the hostler asked, "How was the horse branded?"

"A big dun branded Slash H."

The hostler said promptly, "I remember the horse and I remember him too."

"He stayed at the hotel and likely picked up his horse early."

"Yeah. He woke me about sunup, bought some oats, saddled up and then rode out."

"You see which way he went?" Canning asked carelessly.

"West. He cut across the tracks and I thought he figured to pick up the Indian Bend road."

"How come you remember?" Canning asked curiously.

"It was the horse, I reckon. Never saw a better-looking one, I wanted to watch his gait. I did. Right then, I wished I owned him."

Canning was silent for long moments, thinking. What had sent Hanaway west? What information had he picked up here that had sent him west instead of east or north? Canning asked then, "Did he ask directions? Did he say where he was going?"

"No," the hostler said promptly. "Never talked except to ask for some oats. Acted like a man that knew where he was headed and didn't have to ask the way."

The sheriff came to his decision then. "Know when the next train heading west is due?"

"Well, them trains hauling rail and ties can come through any time. The passenger train should be through in half an hour or less."

Canning pushed away from the table. "I want to leave my horse here. Don't know how long I'll be gone. You want any money down?"

The hostler grinned. "I don't reckon. We always know where we can find you."

Canning nodded. "I'll need the blanket roll from my saddle."

The hostler moved past him and turned into the stable. A minute later he came back with the blanket roll. Accepting it, Canning said, "See you when I get back."

He headed for the depot then. Tramping toward it, he wondered if he wasn't starting out on a wild-goose chase. Still, he thought, the hostler did remember Hanaway and did watch him when he rode out. Hanaway was somewhere west—but there was a hell of a lot of space out there, Canning thought wryly.

At the depot's ticket window he bought a ticket for Indian Bend. Why to there he really didn't know except that the hostler guessed Hanaway was picking up the road to Indian Bend.

He had scarcely stepped out onto the unlit platform when he heard the distant whistle of the train.

145

Presently he picked up the headlights and the train materialized out of the night and coasted to a halt at the station.

It was a mixed train and Canning skirted the two men who were beginning to unload freight and headed for the lamplit passenger car. There were many empty seats in the car and Canning threw his blanket roll onto an empty seat and sat down next to the window. When the train began to move, he put his ticket in his hatband and lay down on the seat, using the blanket roll for a pillow, pulled his hat over his eyes and immediately fell asleep.

He awakened sometime in the night immediately aware that the train was stopped, and was just drifting off to sleep again when a train passed them heading east. After their train jerked into motion and left the siding for the main line, Canning went back to sleep.

It was well past daylight when the train pulled into Indian Bend. Canning, bedroll over his shoulder, stepped down into the cinders, moved away from the train and had his look at the town. It was a sorry little town, he thought. Its main street faced the tracks and consisted of two blocks of false-front stores of both wood and adobe. Canning judged that at least half the stores were boarded up and vacant and for a moment he wondered why in God's name he'd come here. There was scarcely any wagon traffic on the street and, curiously enough, most of the people on the rotting boardwalks were women with shopping baskets. He supposed they were doing their shopping chores before the blasting heat of the day would drive them indoors.

Canning saw a saloon on a corner and made for it. An aproned bartender was rolling beer barrels out to the edge of the boardwalk and stacking them. While Canning wasn't much of a drinking man, the thought of a drink seemed pleasant this morning. His mouth tasted as if a troop of cavalry had ridden through it and, beyond that, his spirits needed lifting by another kind of spirits.

He crossed the street, his blanket roll trailing at his side, and approached the bartender. "Morning," he said. "Can a man get a drink at this hour?"

"Plenty of them do," the bartender said. "Go on in. Be with you in a minute."

Canning went inside and saw two old men, drinks in hand, sitting at a card table. The big room held yet another table beside the scarred bar and deal back bar lined with bottles. Canning nodded to the two old men, they nodded back and he bellied up to the bar. Presently the bartender came in behind the bar and Canning ordered whiskey. The bartender placed the bottle and glass in front of him and Canning poured a small drink into his glass and emptied it, but he did not swallow the whiskey, he rinsed the whiskey around in his mouth for a half minute, then moved over to a spittoon and spat the whiskey into it. Afterward he poured himself a real drink and took a pull at the glass. It was raw and rough whiskey and when he got back his breath he looked at the bartender who was studying his badge. The bartender was a heavy-set man with a broad and florid Irishman's face; the blue eyes that went with that face, however, held a quiet dejection.

"Where is everybody?" Canning asked. "Besides us here, I haven't seen a man on the streets."

"You won't either," the bartender said gloomily. "Anybody that ain't crippled is working at end of track."

"How come you're not?" Canning asked.

"My partner took off and I'm stuck here or I'd be there too."

"You make a living?"

"Barely. When I bought in, the camp was here and we done real good. Men was lined five deep at the bar and we had six dealers working the games the clock around."

Canning looked around the almost bare room and said, "What games?"

"Eh, the games was here, all right. The trouble was the railroad started out laying a mile of track a day.

By the middle of the second week, end of track was so far from here the men was too tired to walk it here and back. Besides, they got gambling and games and women at end of track now."

"Your partner take your games up there?"

"No, he's running a tent saloon. I sold the games to a redheaded gambler that was going to run a tent gambling house."

Canning straightened up, suddenly alert. He remembered Reeves's skill with cards and any gambling game you could name. "You wouldn't remember this redhead's name, would you?"

"Sure, C. D. Williams. Everybody calls him Seedy but he never looked that way. He were duded up like them city gamblers you hear about. Black coat, fancy shirt and black Mexican boots."

Listening to this, Canning was convinced that the bartender was describing Dave Reeves, "Seemed like he had some money?" Canning inquired.

"Well, he paid what I asked for the games and he paid the railroad a good price to haul his gear. You've got to have a stack to run those games, so I'd say he wasn't hurtin'.'"

Canning finished his drink, paid for it and then asked, "Does the railroad take passengers to end of track?"

"Ain't supposed to, but they do. If they see that badge, you won't have no trouble, if that's where you're headed. Any construction train will pick you up. They all stop for water here."

Canning asked where he could get something to eat and the bartender told him and Canning thanked him. Before he had reached the street, Canning knew what he was going to do. He was going to head for end of track on the first train that would take him.

XXIV

When Hanaway was roused from his sleep by a hand on his shoulder, he realized the train was stopped. He looked up to see Ryan smiling down at him. A glance across the aisle showed him that Reeves was sleeping or pretending to.

Ryan said, "Come outside and stretch your legs. I want to talk to you."

Hanaway rose and followed Ryan outside and down the steps. Ryan, lantern in hand, walked past the end of the caboose and halted.

"What are we stopped for?" Hanaway asked.

"Train coming through," Ryan answered. "How's your prisoner?"

"I didn't ask him."

Ryan hesitated and then said, "We got to talking about you up front. How you going to get that redhead to Kittrick?"

"Take him on the next train, I reckon."

"You'll be a sitting duck," Ryan said. "All he's got to do is yell like hell and name you. If you hit him, everybody'll know he named you right, won't they?"

Hanaway sighed and said, "I reckon."

"You think you can keep a carful of people under your gun for twelve hours? Not likely, when there's ten thousand dollars on your head. All it takes is two men with a gun apiece. You go for one and the other one will get you."

"I don't like shooting at people," Hanaway said.

"I know that, but people will be shooting at you."

"You must have an idea."

"I have," Ryan said. "Get that redhead into the car where your horse is. The next eastbound train will pick up the car and leave it on the siding at Junction City."

"Won't that get you in trouble, Ryan?"

Ryan shrugged. "Everybody makes mistakes and that will be one of mine. It ain't as if I stole the car, I just sent it to the wrong place."

Hanaway smiled. "It's kind of like I own this railroad," he said. "Sure, I'll accept your offer."

Ryan nodded. "You untie that redhead while I get another lantern."

They both went back into the caboose. Hanaway roused Reeves and untied him while Ryan took a lantern from the rack and lighted it.

As Hanaway was coiling his lariat, Reeves stretched and rubbed his wrists. "What now?" Reeves asked.

"We're moving to another car."

Ryan came up and handed Hanaway a lighted lantern and then headed for the door.

"Follow him," Hanaway said. Reeves came to his feet unsteadily and, bracing himself against the bunk, followed Ryan out of the door and down the steps.

None of them spoke as Ryan led the way to the car where Hanaway's dun was stalled. Sliding back the door, Ryan climbed into the car and waited for Reeves to climb up and inside. Hanaway put the lantern on the floor and climbed up after him.

They heard a train approaching and heard its whistle. The engineer of their train in turn blew his whistle. It was simply an exchange of greetings in the night that had no significance. When the train was past, headed toward end of track, Ryan put his lantern on the car floor and jumped down.

"You'll get switched around some in Indian Bend. Don't let it bother you. I'll talk to the yard master there, he'll have this car spotted at loading chute in Junction City." Ryan held up his hand and Hanaway shook hands with him. "Good luck, Hanaway. You'll need it."

"With friends like you I don't need any luck," Hanaway said. Ryan waved and headed, lantern in hand, toward the engine. Hanaway slid the door shut and then walked around Reeves and came up to his dun. As he scratched the dun's neck, Hanaway said, "I don't care where you sit or lie, but keep away from that lantern."

Reeves began to prowl at the far end of the car. Just as the train started, Reeves chose a corner to sit where he could brace himself from the lurch and side sway of the car.

Now that Hanaway was assured of safe passage to Junction City, he pondered what he would do with Reeves once he got there. He felt restless and began pacing all over the car, careful to keep away from Reeves.

He tried to remember the Kittrick stage and he recalled that two two-place seats had been ironed to the top of the stage behind the driver for overflow.

He was still pacing when the train pulled into the yarding at Indian Bend. As Ryan had warned him, there was a good deal of bumping and clanging and banging before the car came to rest on the siding where it would be picked up by the eastbound train. When that train would come along, Hanaway didn't know.

He cracked the door, saw it was daylight, then blew the lantern and sat down by the partly opened door and put the lantern beside him. They would very likely need it again tonight.

It was midday before Hanaway heard the train slowly approaching. He closed the door lest one of the crew should spot it and shortly afterward they were again rolling. Opening the door again, he settled down to a day of boredom. He was both hungry and thirsty but he had given the dun the last of the water. In the remaining light he saw Reeves moving out of his corner and coming toward him.

"That's close enough," Hanaway said.

Reeves halted and said, "You got anything to eat or drink?"

"No."

"I haven't eaten since end of track. You know that."

"Neither have I," Hanaway said.

151

Reeves was silent a moment and then said, "I need a doctor, I think you broke my skull."

"I don't see one around, do you?"

Reeves said bitterly, "You'll need one too when Canning's through with you." Reeves went back to his corner.

At full dark Hanaway lighted the lantern again and felt weariness engulf him. He knew if he sat here much longer he'd go to sleep and Reeves would make a try for his gun. He began pacing then, wondering what lay ahead for him and Reeves. Somewhere there had to be some evidence that Reeves murdered Ben, but where was it, what was it and who had it? He supposed Canning would jail him now that Ben was dead. Canning, satisfied he had Ben's killer in jail, wouldn't even try to make a case against Reeves. Hall, of course, could do the leg work while he was in jail, but again, what would Hall be looking for? And while he was looking, Reeves would be free to disappear again.

After weary hours of pacing, Hanaway halted, listening. They were passing a train on the siding, he gathered. The sound of their train was bouncing off the other train in a blasting racket.

An hour later the engine whistled and Hanaway slid the door again. The gray of false dawn was touching the east and Hanaway poked his head out to see if Junction City was in sight.

This was when Reeves hit him, driving into the small of his back with his shoulder. Hanaway was braced by a hand on the door and by a hand on the side of the car, but his feet were driven out from under him. His legs were hanging over the edge of the car and Reeves was pounding his hands with both his own in a savage effort to break Hanaway's grip.

Hanaway was painfully aware that, given enough time, Reeves could break his grip. Unable to get any purchase with his legs, Hanaway did the only thing left for him—he shoved himself back abruptly and at the same time brought his head back. Reeves, his body close to Hanaway's, was so intent on breaking

Hanaway's grip that he made no effort to dodge or halt Hanaway's butting head. It got him full in the mouth and nose and his whole small universe exploded in stars and rockets. He took a step backward, raising his hands to his face. Hanaway turned, fell on his back and, cat-quick, drew his legs in, rolled onto his knees and then came to his feet.

Hanaway drove a fist in his belly and Reeves backpedaled into the opposite door, then slid down to a sitting position, his nose and lips bleeding now.

Hanaway picked up his hat, dusted it off against his trouser leg, put it on and said, "Well, if you don't mind eating your own blood, there's your breakfast."

Again the engine whistled and began to slow down. In the coming dawn, Hanaway could make out the trees and a few outbuildings at the edge of town. He went over to his dun, and backed him out of the stall and saddled him. Reeves was still sitting against the door, handkerchief to his nose and mouth.

The train swerved into a siding and Hanaway said, "Get up and go up to the front of the car."

When Reeves came to his feet and moved, Hanaway opened the door he had been leaning against and saw the switchman signaling just ahead of the stock pens. Slowly the train moved until the loading chute crept up even with the door, then the train halted.

Picking up the dead lantern, Hanaway led his dun to the door and said, "Follow us," to Reeves.

To the switchman standing just outside of the corral Hanaway gave the lantern, saying, "Much obliged, my friend."

The switchman looked at Reeves coming down the floor of the chute and said, "That's a lot of room for two men and a horse."

Hanaway nodded. "Tell Ryan we made it to here, will you?"

At the man's nod, Hanaway moved over to the gate, opened it, led the dun out and then waited for Reeves to pass through. The switchman signaled then and the train began to move again. At the first of the

153

two passenger cars, the switchman climbed aboard, then turned and waved to Hanaway.

When the train pulled past, Hanaway saw they were at the east end of Main Street. There was a lighted cafe opposite the stock pens and Hanaway said to Reeves, "Come on, we'll eat. Only talk to give your order. Anything more and you'll get a bump to match the one you've got now."

There were a couple of cow ponies tied up at the hitch rail in front of the cafe and Hanaway tied the dun between them. Inside two half-drunken cowboys were eating at the far end of the counter. They looked incuriously at the newcomers while Reeves and Hanaway gave their orders.

Breakfast finished, Hanaway paid for them both, ordered Reeves out and, once on the boardwalk, said, "The stage leaves from the feed stable. Better get a move on."

Hanaway swung into the saddle and adjusted his dun's pace to Reeves's walk. When they reached the feed stable the stage was making up. Hanaway dismounted, confirmed that the two overflow seats atop the stage were empty and said to Reeves, "Get on top, back seat. Stay away from the driver."

He watched until Reeves had climbed up and seated himself, then led the dun over to the watering trough. The harnessed teams were now driven through the center way of the stable and were hooked up to the stage. The driver climbed up on the wheel and Reeves reached in his pocket, brought out his wallet and paid. The driver said, "It'll be kind of cold up there."

"I like it," Reeves said. Afterward the driver climbed into the box and headed for the hotel where two men, who looked to be drummers of some sort, climbed into the stage. Hanaway waited behind the stage and, when it pulled out, circled in the wide street and picked up the Kittrick road. He put the dun alongside the stage to be out of the dust.

At midmorning, during the change of teams at Johnson's, Hanaway watered his dun again. Johnson's careless glance at him showed no sign of recognition. Not a strange thing, Hanaway thought, since when he had last talked to Johnson he'd been clean-shaven and now his beard stubble was so heavy that it obscured the jaw line.

The sun was beating down now and Reeves, to protect himself from it, had tied his bloody handkerchief at the four corners and was wearing it like a mob cap. He had spoken to no one and the driver, probably considering him an unfriendly and eccentric man, made no effort at long-distance conversation. In late morning they drove past the Diamond K; on the approach to town Reeves pocketed his improvised sunbonnet.

This entrance into Kittrick would be the most dangerous stage of the journey. While Hanaway knew few people in town, Reeves, after more than a year of residence here, might easily be recognized by any number of people.

When they entered town and were about to pass the feed stable, Hanaway put the stage between him and the loafers who always hung around there. The driver called something to the hostler and got a raucous reply.

When they pulled up at the hotel, Hanaway still had the stage between him and the veranda loafers. He pulled close to the stage and said to Reeves, "Get down on this side, then head for the courthouse."

Submissively, Reeves climbed down and headed for the corner they had just passed. Hanaway rode beside him as far as the corner and breathed a sigh of relief. Nobody had spoken to either Reeves or himself.

Now Hanaway steeled himself for what he was about to meet. If Canning were in his office, there was a perfectly good chance he'd pull a gun. Where it would go from there, Hanaway didn't know. Canning would have to get a message to Hall and from there it would be mostly up to Hall.

Hanaway ordered Reeves to make a half circle of the courthouse and stop at the wagon shed. Once there, Hanaway saw there were two horses tied inside out of the sun. He dismounted and put his dun alongside them. Then together, he and Reeves went to the rear door of the courthouse. Hannaway waited for Reeves to go first and then took a deep breath. The door of the sheriff's office was open and Reeves walked through it, Hanaway two steps behind him. There at the desk, face to the wall, was white-haired Marshal Barnard. At the sound of footsteps the marshal looked around and then pure shock came into his face. He rose slowly and said to Hanaway, "Good God, man, are you crazy?" He skirted the two of them, then closed and locked the door.

"Morning Marshal. I suppose I'm looking for Canning. Is he around?"

"He's out looking for you. I guess I'm the man you want. First I got something to show you." He went over to his desk, took a piece of paper from the tall stack, came back to Hanaway and extended it saying, "I'm forging Canning's signature on these and sending them out. Read it."

Hanaway did. It was a reward dodger and it gave an accurate description of him, his name, the brand of the dun, his probable age and a warning that he was armed and very dangerous. Hanaway looked up at the marshal. "This posted all over town?"

"Hell, yes," Barnard said.

"Well, I reckon you're the first one to claim the reward, Marshal, but I don't think you'll have it long."

"I wouldn't take it, but why wouldn't I have it long?"

Hanaway gestured to Reeves. "Because there's Ben Kittrick's killer."

The marshal's pale and wise old eyes regarded Hanaway for long moments. "You got any proof, Hanaway?"

"No, but I will have."

"What do you want me to do with him?" the marshal asked.

Hanaway said, "Just what I'd do if I were in your

boots. I'd lock him up until the sheriff got back here. After all, the murder of Ben Kittrick happened in the county and it's his case to prosecute."

The marshal, still watching Hanaway, said softly, "Tell me more."

Reeves spoke for the first time, and angrily. "This killer can't have me thrown in jail! He's got no authority!"

Barnard looked at him with distaste and then his glance shifted to Hanaway, who said mildly, "Look at it this way, Marshal. You'd be a fool to turn Reeves loose while Canning's gone. You should hold him for Canning to question. Turn him loose and you've exceeded your authority. Even if Canning can't pry anything out of him, at least he deserves the chance to try. After all, he's elected, while you're only appointed marshal and deputy marshal."

A glint of amusement came into the marshal's eyes, but his sober, serious face showed only concern as he said, "I never thought of that. I'm only the hired hand while he's the boss."

"Exactly," Hanaway said gravely. "The decision is his to make, not yours."

Reeves said hotly, "Are either of you lawyers? You can't pick a man up off the street and throw him in jail because someone said he killed a man!"

"Just like I can't let loose a man accused of murder. That's up to the sheriff, like you heard. Why, I'd lose my job if I let you go without he saw you first."

"But who's accusing me of murder?" Reeves asked hotly. "The murderer himself! Why have you got reward posters out for him? Why is the sheriff hunting him?"

"Why, he's just turned himself in," the marshal said blandly. "If he was the real murderer, would he come back to stand trial?"

At last Marshal Barnard had it, Hanaway thought. Maybe he had it from the very first when he and Reeves had walked in.

"Then you're going to lock me up?" Reeves asked hotly.

Barnard nodded. "I'm going to lock you both up—him for murder, you for questioning by the sheriff."

"I want you to get hold of Kelso for me and damn quick!"

Barnard shook his head. "I'd have to go all the way to Kansas City to find him."

"Then Hall, get Hall," Reeves said angrily.

"He's already my lawyer," Hanaway said.

"Then who in hell can get me out of jail?" Reeves demanded.

"Why, nobody except the sheriff, Reeves." Barnard moved past them to the door saying, "Hanaway, you stay here. Reeves, you come along." He unlocked the door, stepped aside and stood waiting.

Reeves turned to Hanaway. "You won't get away with it, Hanaway," he said bitterly. "If I was turned loose right now, I'd stay around here to see you hung." He moved toward the door and headed for the cellblock below.

Hanaway smiled now. Marshal Barnard had played the role of a hick-town thickheaded lawman afraid of losing his job to perfection. Hands on hips, Hanaway began to prowl the room. When he came to Canning's sign on the door he read it and smiled again. He heard Marshal Barnard's footsteps on the stairs and then the marshal came in and closed the door behind him. Turning, the marshal looked at Hanaway, shook his head and smiled. He gestured to the chair beside the sheriff's desk and took the swivel chair.

Hanaway sat down. The marshal said, "I've seen plenty of sandys run in my life, but that beats them all. How did you think that one up?"

"Pure panic," Hanaway said. "I was expecting to see Canning here. When I saw you, I figured between the two of us we could swing it."

The marshal nodded. "I was a little slow there at first, but then I'm a little old too." He locked his fingers behind his head, tilted his chair back and said, "Now you've got him, what will you do with him?"

"I wish I knew," Hanaway said. "I think the first thing to do is see Hall. Am I safe on the streets?"

"Anything but," Barnard said. "I don't know how you made it to here." He rose and picked up his hat. "I'll send Hall over here and then take down them dodgers. Better leave the door closed."

Within ten minutes there was a knock on the door and Harry Hall stepped in, a smile on his face. Hanaway rose and they shook hands. Hall slacked down in the sheriff's chair and said, "The marshal told me what happened. You'd make a good crooked lawyer, Hanaway."

"How's Carrie? How's Neva?"

"Worried about you," Hall said.

Hanaway smiled wryly. "I was a little worried about me too."

"Barnard left me to tell them you're here. They should be here any time," Hall said, and then spoke what was really on his mind. "Get anything out of Reeves?"

"Nothing except trouble and a cursing out."

"Well, we've got him, but what good does it do? I've talked with Anna Reeves. She still says she was getting ready for bed when Ben was shot. She didn't see anything or hear anything except the shot. Neither did Lupe or José. Where'd you find Reeves?"

Hanaway told him of his talk with Johnson who told him of Reeves's curiosity about the railroad construction camp at end of track. Hanaway said his hunch had proved correct when he found Reeves there. He told of Ryan and the help the train crews gave him in getting Reeves here.

Hall listened in silence and when Hanaway was finished shook his head. "What in hell do we do with him, Hanaway?"

Hanaway scratched his cheek; it made a rasping sound against his beard stubble and itching cheek. He asked then, "Is Anna Reeves still at Diamond K?" At Hall's nod, he asked, "Why is she? Hasn't Carrie told her to move?"

"Carrie says she's probably waiting to hear from Reeves."

159

"Could you find out if she's hurting for money? Is she paying her bills and wages for the help?"

Hall frowned. "I could, but why?"

"I don't reckon Reeves left her with money. He likely figured Ben had taken care of that."

Hall shrugged. "Maybe. I'll ask around. But if she's broke, what does that prove?"

Hanaway thought a moment, then said, "It's just a feeling I've got, Harry, but this is the way it goes. I think Anna knows, without any kind of proof, that Reeves killed Ben. She knows I had no reason to kill him, and Reeves had every reason to kill him."

"Ben stole Anna and fired him."

Hanaway nodded. "I'm guessing Reeves kept all the money Ben paid him. Anna didn't see any of it, because Ben bought her anything she wanted." He paused. "All right so far?" At Hall's nod, Hanaway went on. "She's free now and I'd guess broke. Reeves knows that. They made a good team once, so why not try it again, Reeves would think."

"That's possible."

Hanaway nodded.

"What are you getting at?" Hall asked.

"Let's buy her," Hanaway said. "We pay her what Reeves will never give her—half of what Ben paid Reeves for her. But not before she gives us proof Reeves killed Ben. That will come out in her testimony at Reeves's trial for murder."

Hall pondered before saying, "Two things wrong. One: does she hate him enough to testify against him?"

"When Reeves killed Ben he robbed her of a fortune."

"All right. Number two: where do we get the money to pay her?"

"I've turned down an offer of thirty thousand for my spread up north, thanks to old Jeff Kittrick. I could sell it for that today."

"And ride the grub line afterward?"

"Sure. But the point is, I'd be riding it. I wouldn't be dead, or rotting in jail."

"Yeah," Hall said softly. "It's worth a try, but what if Anna really doesn't know Reeves killed Ben and Reeves will never tell her?"

"With that much money at stake she'll get it out of him some way."

"We hope," Hall said glumly.

They heard swift footfalls in the corridor and both men were rising as Carrie, at a run, came through the door, Neva behind her. Without any hesitation at all, Carrie came into Hanaway's arms and kissed him on the mouth, then hugged him to her. Neva waited until they had separated, then extended her hand, which Hanaway took. Both girls looked beautiful, Hanaway thought, but Carrie was radiant with joy.

"Marshal Barnard says he has Reeves locked up. Where did you find him and how did you get him here?" Carrie asked.

Hanaway motioned the girls to the chairs, while Hall leaned against the desk. Hanaway was heartily sick of having to tell his story for the third time in an hour, but as he warily circled the room, he told it again. He told, what was for him the truth, that Ryan, instead of collecting ten thousand dollars head money on him, had instead worked the impossible. He, in effect, was Reeves's captor.

While the girls were still questioning him, Marshal Barnard came in. He sat on the cot in the corner and listened to Hanaway finish. Carrie shook her head. "So instead of shooting you or capturing you he got you to Junction City. There's a man I'm going to meet, because I'll never see another one like him."

She looked at Marshal Barnard then. "Marshal, would you bring over your prisoner and have supper with us tonight?"

Barnard said slyly, "Which one?" They all laughed and the marshal said, "Be glad to."

XXV

It was midmorning when the marshal, Hall and Hanaway rode into the Diamond K and tied their horses at the corral, afterward walking up to the house. Last night at the Kittrick house it was agreed that Hall should be there when Hanaway talked with Anna Reeves. The marshal was necessary because Hanaway was legally his prisoner, but they all agreed he should stay outside for fear of scaring Anna into silence.

When Lupe answered their knock, she looked surprised, then stepped aside. Hall and Hanaway entered and Hanaway asked, "Will Miss Reeves see us, please?"

Lupe disappeared into the bedroom wing, then reappeared, gestured for them to be seated, and moved through the dining room into the kitchen.

Both men had barely seated themselves when Anna Reeves appeared in the doorway. She halted there as both men rose. Hanaway had seen her only on the night he broke Ben's nose. With her ashen hair and dark skin she was even more beautiful than he remembered. She was wearing a severe light blue dress that only underlined her slim but full figure.

She looked from one to the other and then returned her glance to Hanaway. She said then, "If you're who I think you are, what are you doing in this house?"

"The marshal is just outside. I'm under arrest and he's my guard, so don't be afraid." He gestured to Hall. "This is my lawyer, Harry Hall."

Anna came into the room then and asked Hanaway bluntly. "What do you want?"

"Well, first to sit down. This may take some time."

"Not much of mine, I assure you," When neither man answered, she said grudgingly, "All right, sit down." She seated herself on the sofa and watched them seat themselves.

When Hall was seated, he asked conversationally, "What do you hear from Dave, Miss Reeves?"

"Nothing. He's in California," Anna said guardedly.

"No. He's in jail here. His cell is next to Hanaway's," Hall said.

The shock in her face was real; her hand came up to her throat. "That just can't be," she exclaimed.

Hall said, "The marshal's outside. Want to ask him?"

"But what's he done?" Anna demanded.

Hanaway said, "He killed Ben Kittrick. You know that and I know that."

"But *you* killed Ben! There's evidence you did! There's even a reward out for you!"

Hall asked quietly, "How's your money holding out, Miss Reeves? Did Dave send you your share?"

"My share of what?" Anna asked uncertainly.

"Of the fifty-three thousand dollars Ben paid him in salary and gifts."

"Oh that. Of course he did," Anna replied.

"Where is it?" Hall persisted.

"Why is that any of your business?" Anna asked coldly.

"Just curious," Hall said softly. "You're not paying your bills, Miss Reeves. You're not paying your help either. You're sending out your jewels to be sold. Now that Reeves is in jail, I think the Kittrick sisters will ask you to leave this place. Ben never gave it to you. Do you think Dave will lease it for you?"

Anna rose and said coldly, "I'll ask you to leave. Get out!"

"Not quite yet," Hanaway said, not moving. When Anna glared at him and started to speak, Hanaway held up his hand, palm out. Her scene shattered, Anna could only watch him, as if dreading what was coming.

"You're in some trouble, Miss Reeves—or whatever your name is. You're close to broke and Dave won't help you, because he can't. He's going to hang."

Anna sat down ever so slowly. "How do you know that?"

"Because if they don't hang him, I'll kill him," Hanaway said. "So there's no way he can help you."

Anna watched him for long seconds, then said, "You're trying to tell me something but I don't understand what it is."

"How would you like half of what Dave gouged out of Ben? Say thirty thousand dollars?"

Anna regarded him loosely. "What do I have to do to get it? Live with you?"

"No," Hanaway said.

He let her ponder that and when she said what she next said—"Prove you have it"—he knew he'd won.

Hanaway started to speak but Hall rose, came over to her, extended a packet of paper and said, "Six hundred shares of Consolidated stock, negotiable anywhere in the territory. Worth a little over thirty thousand dollars." Hall looked at Hanaway who could not hide his amazement. Hall smiled and then looked at Anna who was examining a certificate.

She raised her head now and said, "What do I have to do to earn them?"

"Get an admission from Dave that he killed Ben Kittrick and testify to it in court," Hall said.

Anna was silent, looking from one man to the other. Hanaway knew what she was feeling because her pretty face told him—shame that he and Hall thought she could be bought, and a transparent greed for this much money.

"What do you owe him?" Hall prodded. "You were set with Ben for life and Reeves killed him. Reeves has treated you without care, consideration and conscience, so what do you owe him for ruining your life?"

Anna shook her head and said miserably, "I can't kill a man."

"He killed your man, didn't he? He's put you on the streets, hasn't he?"

Anna nodded, looking at her hands folded in her lap.

Hall walked over to his chair and sat down. Now decision came into Anna's face. She rose, said, "I'll be back," and went back into the bedroom wing.

Hanaway said, "You got those certificates from Carrie."

Hall nodded. "Yesterday afternoon while you were sleeping. This called for cash in hand, not a deed to a ranch she's never seen. You can settle it with Carrie later."

Anna Reeves came into the room then, an envelope in her hand. Both men rose. She went to the sofa and picked up the pack of certificates. "Can I sell these?" she asked.

"You only looked at the front of them," Hall said. "Look on the back and you'll find they're signed over to you by Carrie Kittrick. Present them to me and I'll give you cash for them."

Anna asked suspiciously, "Why you? What have you got to do with Consolidated?"

"I'm its president, as of last night."

She looked at Hanaway, and he nodded. "As a small shareholder I helped vote him in."

Then, almost reluctantly, she came over to Hanaway and extended the envelope. He took it and read the address as Hall came up beside him. Taking out the letter inside, Hanaway held it so Hall could read it with him. They read it and looked at each other; Hall shrugged and Hanaway looked at Anna and asked, "What's this supposed to mean?"

"Look at the date of his letter. Look at the date of the Indian Bend postmark. Ben wasn't dead when Dave wrote that letter. How would Dave know Ben was shot if he didn't shoot him and thought he killed him?"

Hanaway and Hall checked the dates and saw that Anna was right. Hanaway gave both letter and envelope to Hall, then moved across the room to the outside door. When he opened it, Marshal Barnard was facing the corral; he looked over his shoulder at Hanaway.

"Come in, Marshal. We have a present for you."

165

Sheriff Wes Canning, his horse tied to the stage's boot, stepped down into the hot dust of Kittrick's Main Street in front of the hotel. He was tired and frustrated and mad. His trip to end of track had led him to a dead end. As near as he could piece together the information he'd got from Reeves's dealers, the guy ropes of Reeves's gambling tent had been cut, the tent set afire, Reeves's sleeping tent entered and Reeves was gone. Nobody knew where he was gone or why. Nobody he had talked to at camp could verify that Hanaway had been there.

Canning had ridden back to Indian Bend on the night train. The trainmaster, a man named Ryan, had admitted it was perfectly possible for one or two men to have stolen a ride since the train was made up of nothing but empties. At Indian Bend neither the yardmaster, nor the station agent, nor the conductor of the train he took east out of Indian Bend were of any help, and that was when Canning gave up.

He took his horse down to the stable, asked that he be fed and washed down, then headed afoot for the courthouse. All this travel these days and nights had been a complete waste of time.

At the courthouse he found his office door locked. After letting himself in, he looked around and spotted a neat stack of reward dodgers atop the desk. After reading one and finding it satisfactory, he knew he would be spending the next couple of days signing and mailing them.

He was hungry now and he left the office, closing the door behind him. He was heading down the corridor when he hauled up. He'd better check the jail, he thought, in case there were some prisoners to feed. Retracing his steps, he went down the jail stairway and halted abruptly. Dave Reeves was sitting on his cell cot watching the stairways. As Canning hit the corridor floor, Reeves rose.

"Dave! What the hell are you doing in there?"

Standing at the cell door, Reeves told the sheriff of his kidnapping from end of track by Hanaway. He also told of Hanaway's trumped-up charge that he had killed Ben and of Hanaway's persuading Marshal Barnard to lock him up until Canning arrived.

"The whole thing is a pure frameup," Reeves finished. "I'm in here illegally and you know it, Wes. Now let me out."

Canning's face held a tight anger. "Let's get this straight, Dave. You're telling me Hanaway talked the old boy into holding you?" At Reeves's nod, Canning said, "On what charge?"

"No charge. He just said he'd hold me until you had a chance to question me."

Canning reached in his pocket and brought out a key, and Reeves went back to the cot and picked up his frock coat. "All right, I've questioned you," Canning said. "I'm sorry this had to happen, Dave. You could probably sue hell out of me and win, but you've got to believe I don't know about any of this, let alone give orders for your lock up."

He unlocked the door and Reeves stepped through it. "Did the old boy free Hanaway?"

"No. He was locked up last night. This morning the marshal came and took him out."

"Know where?"

"Got no idea," Reeves said.

"I'll have one pretty quick," Canning said grimly. "Let's go eat. I'm hungry."

"Just one thing, Wes. Hanaway took away my gun. It's in your office."

"All right."

They went back to the office. Canning rummaged around the drawers of his desk and found Reeves's derringer and gave it to him. On the way to the hotel Canning told Reeves of these last days and how he'd traced him to end of track, then lost the trail. Reeves, in turn, told him where he could have picked it up—the depot at Junction City, the restaurant, the stage driver. Ryan had lied to him; he himself hadn't been sharp enough to catch the lie.

They had reached Main Street, and Canning's amber eyes were searching. Marshal Barnard, along with Hanaway, had to be somewhere. Hall's office? The

Kittrick house? Consolidated? Diamond K? Hell, he was hungry. Time enough later to track the Marshal down.

And then he saw Anna Reeves, accompanied by Harry Hall, come out of the open doorway of the bank. He halted and put out his arm to stop Reeves. They watched as Hanaway and Marshal Barnard followed Anna and Hall.

"Jackpot," Canning said softly and started across the street, Reeves following. By the time they had waited for a team and wagon to pass, Hall, Anna, Hanaway and the marshal had halted and were talking. It was Hanaway who first saw the sheriff and Reeves approaching.

"Here comes your boss, Marshal," Hanaway said. The three of them turned in the direction Hanaway was looking.

Canning and Reeves came up to them and halted in the street as Canning said, "Well, well. Walking the dog, are you, Marshal?"

The marshal looked at Reeves, then Canning. "Just like you. Why's he out?"

"Why was he ever in?" Canning countered angrily.

"Because he killed Ben Kittrick," Barnard said.

"A jury tell you that?"

"No. You might say Reeves told me. He told you too," Barnard said. He reached in his shirt pocket, brought out Reeves's letter and handed it to Canning. "Read it, then pay attention to the date of the letter and the date of the postmark. Then remember the date Ben Kittrick died."

Canning read the letter. While he was pondering it, Hanaway watched Reeves, who was looking at Anna with the purest hatred. Hanaway saw Reeves's hand move slowly toward his coat pocket and disappear in it. When Reeves's hand started to lift, his eyes still on Anna, Hanaway moved. He turned to Anna beside him, put his hands on her shoulder and shoved her sideways. She left her feet, screamed while falling as Reeves, derringer out, fired the gun at her.

The marshal had been watching Canning's face. At

Anna's wail, his glance raked across to Reeves beside Canning. Barnard went for his own gun as Reeves raised his and shot. The marshal's own shot came as an instant echo of Reeves's shot. Reeves was slammed flat on his back in the dust. Both his hands started for his chest, faltered and dropped to the dust too.

Hanaway, who had dropped and rolled as he pushed Anna, now rose and came over to her and gave her a hand up. Reeves's bullet had missed. Hall stood rooted beside the marshal, Canning still had the letter in his hand. As he moved over to Reeves, he looked down at him and said, "So."

XXVI

When Hanaway stopped talking and pacing the flag-stones under the big cottonwood at the Kittrick house, he halted in front of Carrie.

She said, "So now you can go home. No reward dodgers out and the sheriff's satisfied. Ben's killer is dead, and so is Ben." She shook her head. "You must be sorry you ever knew Uncle Jeff or any of us Kittricks. We've been nothing but trouble to you."

"Trouble I asked for. Trouble I owed. Trouble I'm glad I had."

"Glad?" Carrie echoed. "You can't be serious."

"How else would I have met you?"

Carrie looked intently at him. "Is that important to you?"

"Just the most important thing that ever happened to me." He reached out and she extended her hands and he pulled her to her feet and kissed her. Afterwards he said, "I hope it's important to you too."

Carrie smiled. "I'll have to give that some thought—about a lifetime's."

FROM THE PRODUCER OF
THE KENT FAMILY CHRONICLES
WAGONS WEST—VOLUME II

NEBRASKA
by Dana Fuller Ross

Here is a special preview
of the exciting opening pages of the
second book in this sweeping saga of the
men and women whose lives were
caught up in America's westward drive.

1

Heavy clouds, thick and black, ominous in their intensity, blew eastward from the Rocky Mountains across the Great Plains wilderness, obscuring the moon and stars. The night air had been cool, but the ground was still warm from the early autumn sun that had shone down on Missouri the previous day, so a white mist, as impenetrable as a bale of cotton, rose from the broad waters of the great Missouri River, bathing the whole area in a blanket of swirling mists.

High on the bluffs of the eastern bank of the river, a short distance from the frontier village of Independence, stood the symbols of the future. Wagon after wagon arranged in a circle. Flexible wooden hoops were looped upward over their sides and covered with thick canvas to protect the inhabitants from the elements. There were scores of wagons, hundreds of men, women and children in the caravan, all of them asleep. They were the first pioneers who would blaze a path to the Pacific Ocean and, in the decades to come, would be followed by thousands of others making their way to the Oregon Territory and California.

Some had already traveled all the way from

the Eastern seaboard, to be joined by others along the way in a daring venture unique in the annals of the history of the young United States. Only optimists, only Americans, would have dreamed such dreams of the future or dared to make such a long trek into the unknown.

Inside the circle, the horses and oxen were asleep, too, as were the dogs. None stirred.

There seemed to be nothing to fear. Independence was a sturdy little community of ranch owners and farmers—people who took the law into their own hands when need be because no other law existed at this remote outpost. Bloodshed was not unknown, but violence occurred infrequently.

No one in the wagon train heard the two boats being rowed across the Missouri from the west bank with muffled oars. No one saw the little craft hauled ashore, beached and made secure. Certainly no one in the train knew that six armed men, frontier drifters who preyed on fur trappers or isolated farm owners, were finding the train a target too tempting to be left in peace. There were animals to steal, valuables to snatch—prizes for desperadoes who placed small value on human life.

The six men crept up the hill, pistols and knives in their hands. A shepherd dog stretched outside one of the wagons awakened and raised its pointed ears. The bandits crept closer, struggling quietly as they made their way up the palisade.

One member of the wagon train stirred. Tall and lean, dressed in the buckskins, he was sound asleep one moment, completely awake and alert the next. He reached for his long rifle automatically and rose to his feet with effortless grace, in a single move.

A glance told him the mist was too thick for him to see, so he listened intently, his head cocked to one side. Then a faint, grim smile appeared on his face. Moving silently, with the experience of one who had spent years as a hunter, trapper and guide in the Rockies, he went quickly to several key wagons.

In almost no time he was joined by a motley group of men, carrying rifles. The trio followed the man in buckskins to the lip of the bluff. No one could see much more than a few feet ahead—certainly no one in the group could hear anything untoward. Within a few seconds they were joined by an Indian brave, also clad in buckskins—a warrior who almost casually notched an arrow in his bow. Like the man in buckskins, he had no need to see the approaching menace.

The marauders came still closer. They were no more than fifty feet from the top of the bluff. A broad smile appeared on the face of the man in buckskins. There was no doubt that he thoroughly enjoyed the challenge of danger. He didn't need to speak; his companions had traveled far with him, and knew what was expected of them.

Now the robbers were no more than five

yards from the lip of the palisade, almost within reach of their goal. The man in buckskins nodded, almost laconically, and four rifles spoke simultaneously, the weapons deliberately fired over the heads of the approaching foe.

The startled bandits paused, then turned and fled down the steep slope, sliding and stumbling, falling and scrambling as they raced to the safety of their waiting boat.

Now it was the Indian's turn. He sent arrow after arrow toward the retreating enemies. The bandits saw the arrows dropping among them and increased their wild pace as they dragged their boat into the water and rowed off to safety.

The man in buckskins listened, heard the fading sound of oars, and nodded. His companions turned and strolled back to their wagons for another hour of sleep. He rolled himself in his blanket. The Indian followed his example. Within a few minutes they had drifted back to sleep.

The ears of the shepherd dog drooped again, and the mist was still thick. The men, women and children of the train were deep in slumber. Even those who had awakened briefly had mistaken the firearms volley for a crack of thunder.

The wagon train was secure.

As always Cathy van Ayl looked lovely as she emerged from her wagon, and as always she seemed unaware of her beauty. She paused on the back step to tuck some stray strands of her long, blonde hair under her sunbonnet, then tightened the sash of her dimity dress. She looked like a young girl in her teens rather than a widow of twenty-three, but that innocence wasn't accidental. Her elderly husband, Otto, a miserly farmer from Long Island who had died in a raid on the wagon train had never been affectionate toward her.

Cathy finished primping just as Whip Holt, the hired guide and wagonmaster of the Oregon-bound caravan, came into view. Tall and sinewy in his buckskins, he was armed, as usual, with a brace of pistols and the long bullwhip, wrapped about his middle, that gave him his name. His skin was leathery after a lifetime of exposure to the outdoors, and his eyes were hard. Then he saw Cathy, and when he grinned at her he suddenly looked younger than twenty-nine.

She smiled at him in return, her heart skipping a beat. When her husband was alive she'd had to conceal her interest in Whip, but all that had changed. Now she had no reason beyond her own sense of discretion to hide the way she felt.

Certainly Whip made no secret of his own feelings. "Morning, ma'am," he called, sauntering toward her.

"You're wearing a new buckskin shirt and trousers, I see," she said politely.

He was startled that she noticed what he was wearing. "Well, you know how it is. I

get restless just sitting around Independence
while we put in supplies and wait for the
new folks joining us to show up. So one day
I took me hunting." He cleared his throat
awkwardly. "You look mighty nice, all
dressed up for a day in the city."

Cathy couldn't help laughing. Certainly no
one else in 1837 would dream of referring to
the frontier town of Independence, Missouri,
as a "city." The last outpost of civilization
east of the Great Plains, it was visited by
trappers, hunters and traders bringing their
furs from the Rocky Mountains to the East.
Now, with other wagon trains scheduled to
follow Whip's caravan across the wilderness
to the fertile Oregon country, Independence
promised to develop into a major supply center.

"I told my sister I'd buy some things in
town for her and bring them along tonight."

Only a few days earlier Cathy's older sister,
Claudia, had been married to Sam Brent-
wood, the former leader of the wagon train.
The couple would remain in Independence to
establish a supply depot, sponsored by Sam's
mentors, former President of the United
States Andrew Jackson, and John Jacob Astor,
a fur baron, leader of a group of wealthy
businessmen who were encouraging the
American settlement of the Oregon territory.

"Claudia and Sam asked me to supper tonight, too," Whip said, and shifted in embarrassment. "I—I wasn't so sure I wanted to

go, seeing as how I don't sit me down at a table indoors very often. But if you're going, ma'am, I'll be happy to escort you."

"I'd like that," Cathy said. She smiled again before turning away, then added, "I'm not really dressed up, you know. All I own are a few dresses like this, except for the old woolen things I wear on the trail."

"Could you use a doeskin dress, ma'am?"

"I'd love it, Whip." Cathy hesitated. "But I wouldn't want you to think I was hinting."

"No matter. Stalking Horse," he said, referring to his close friend, a Cherokee scout, "has been pestering me to try our hands at hunting again, so I reckon I'll have some skins for you by the time we push off."

Cathy thanked him, discomfited by his generosity, then left the circle of wagons. Directly ahead, beyond the bend in the Missouri River, stood the limitless wilderness that stretched across the Great Plains, the Rocky Mountains and, on the far side of the Continental Divide, yet another chain of mountains which the wagon train would have to cross before reaching Oregon.

Otto van Ayl had given his wife no choice and had been determined to go to Oregon. But the widowed Cathy had an alternative and was free to make up her own mind. Claudia and Sam had offered her a home with them, right here in Independence. And she wouldn't be dependent on their charity, either. Her wagon was as solid as any made in

New England, where they had originated in the days prior to the War of Independence. The four horses which pulled it were strong, surefooted and healthy. She could get a substantial sum for the wagon and team if she decided to stay behind when the train moved out. In addition, Otto had left her the fortune he had saved in a lifetime of miserly living, two thousand dollars in gold. When they started on the journey; Otto had concealed the money beneath a false floor in the wagon, but after his death, at Claudia and Sam's insistence, she had moved it for safekeeping to the enormous special wagon where the caravan's medicines, extra weapons and emergency rations were stored.

So Cathy was wealthy, at least by the standards of the emigrants who were heading out to Oregon. Certainly she could pay for her keep if she decided to stay with her sister and new brother-in-law. Fortunately she wouldn't have to make up her mind for a few days; there were influences pulling her in both directions.

Because of Whip she wanted to go on. But she was a grown woman, not a romantic adolescent, and she couldn't allow her interest in him to become too great a factor. It was true, however, that she believed in finishing what she started, and if any of the stories she had heard about Oregon were true, it was heaven on earth.

Tugging her in the opposite direction was the knowledge that powerful forces were at work trying to prevent the American settlers from reaching their destination. The ownership of the Oregon country was in dispute, with both the United States and Great Britain claiming it. A British agent, Henry St. Clair, had already made several violent attempts to halt the train, even inspiring a vicious attack on the caravan by Army deserters. Although that last attempt had failed, several members of the company had been killed. And the pioneers would not have been comforted, had they known the thoughts that were still going through St. Clair's head. By God, he promised himself, they're not going to beat me! Hell or high water, I'm going to stop that damn wagon train!

But the British attempt to sabotage the train wasn't the only one. Imperial Russia wanted to stop them from reaching Oregon, too. Russians had been the first to settle in Oregon. Although international pressures had forced the czar seemingly to abandon his claim, the government in St. Petersburg was actually doing no such thing. Cathy was one of the few members of the caravan who knew that attempts had been made by the *Cheka*, the czar's secret police, to blackmail a lovely, frontier-wise girl named Tonie Mell into working for them. Tonie's parents, whom she hadn't seen since early childhood, were still in Russia. She had been told they wouldn't be allowed to join her unless she committed acts of sabotage against the train. Thanks to her own courage and the help of

Sam and Whip, she had outsmarted them. But it was fair to assume that the Russians would try again.

In addition, there were terrifying rumors among the settlers about the hostile Indian tribes in the wilderness ahead. There were some pessimists who predicted that every last man, woman and child in the train would be murdered. But Cathy refused to believe such rubbish. No matter how great the menace of Indians might become, she had unbounded faith in Whip Holt's abilities. She had seen him in action, and she was confident he would lead the band of settlers, already four hundred strong and growing every day, to their Oregon destination in safety. She was convinced that no Indians could prevent Whip from reaching his goal—for that matter, neither could the British and Russians.

Tonight, perhaps, she would discuss the decision with her sister; it might clarify her own thinking.

The wagon train had made camp outside Independence, where the horses and oxen could graze, and Cathy headed toward the town. She passed log cabins and houses of whitewashed clapboard. Until the past year, Independence had been little more than a village. But now it boasted two general stores, a stable, and, on its main street, two brothels and at least a dozen taverns and saloons. When Sam and Claudia finished making changes in the ranch, their property would become the principal supply depot for later wagon trains.

The depot would sell both horses and oxen, as well as spare wheels, axles and yokes. Thanks to Claudia's experience on the long march from New York to Missouri, she planned to put in a full supply of such provisions as bacon, flour, beans and sugar—the staples that every immigrant family needed on the trek across the continent. Thanks to the generosity of Astor and his associates, as well as the official encouragement of President Martin Van Buren, Sam would have enough funds to put in a stock of firearms, gunpowder and ammunition, too.

The morning sun was warm, almost hot, the breeze was gentle and it seemed more like summer than the beginning of autumn. It was small wonder that Whip was eager to start the march across the plains as soon as possible. Cathy knew from her own experience in the past six months that the caravan could travel ten to twelve miles per day in good weather, but that progress was slowed to a crawl when it rained. When the rains were very heavy it sometimes became necessary to call a complete halt.

Pondering her decision, paying scant attention to her immediate surroundings, Cathy was suddenly aroused from her reverie by the sound of a man's harsh, deep voice.

"That there one is the prettiest I've seen since we got to this town. I claim her!"

"Like hell you do," another man, replied. "Maybe we'll draw lots for her, all of us, or maybe we'll leave the choice up to her. We got to be fair about this."

The startled Cathy saw eight or nine men who had just emerged from a tavern directly ahead. In spite of the early hour, they had been drinking heavily. Some of them were dressed in shabby linsey-woolsey and others in worn, greasy buckskins. They had not shaved for days and their hair was dirty and unkempt. All were armed with skinning knives, as well as either pistols or rifles.

These were the men Whip and Sam contemptuously referred to as "frontier scum," opportunists who earned a precarious living. Sometimes they bought furs from trappers down on their luck and sold them to traders. Sometimes they did odd jobs for local homesteaders. They were as unsavory as they were unreliable, and Cathy blamed herself for failing to see them in time to avoid them.

But she had little time for regrets. The group had spread across the road, blocking her path, and she was afraid, judging by their leers, that they would maul her if she tried to crowd past them. But she might be in even worse trouble if she turned and tried to flee; certainly that would encourage them in their game. There were no other pedestrians, no riders in sight, so it would be useless to call for help.

The best way to handle the situation, she decided, would be to keep moving forward, remaining calm, and ignoring the brutes. She was tempted to pick up her flounced skirt and run, but instead she continued to walk at the same, even pace, her head high.

One of her tormentors muttered something, and the group quickly surrounded the girl. The man with the rasping voice, appointing himself the spokesman, grinned at her. "You look like you need some lovin'," he said, "so take your pick."

"Let me pass, please." Cathy knew no escape was possible, but made an effort to speak calmly.

"Don't put on no airs with us, girlie," another declared. "You women up the road charge enough, so it's high time you give us somethin' free."

The stunned Cathy suddenly realized they had mistaken her for a girl from one of the brothels. Certainly they were in no mood— perhaps in no condition—to heed her denials. She was in real danger and she didn't know how to escape.

Follow the lives of Whip and Cathy, Claudia and Sam, and all those people who continue the hazardous journey from Independence to Nebraska. Their ultimate destination—Oregon. Read the complete book, to be available July 1, wherever Bantam Books are sold.